JEDI QUEST

THE DANGEROUS GAMES

JEDI QUEST

CHOSEN BY FATE.
DESTINED FOR CONFLICT.

JEDI QUEST

BY JUDE WATSON

THE DANGEROUS GAMES

SCHOLASTIC INC.

New York   Toronto   London   Auckland   Sydney
Mexico City   New Delhi   Hong Kong   Buenos Aires

www.starwars.com
www.starwarskids.com
www.scholastic.com

ISBN 0-439-33919-7

Cover art by Alicia Buelow and David Mattingly.

12 11 10 9 8 7 6 5 4 3 2 1   2 3 4 5 6 7/0

Printed in the U.S.A.
First Scholastic printing, August 2002

The spacelanes of the planet Euceron were jammed with vehicles. In the upper atmosphere, large transports and sleek passenger liners chugged in orbit. Despite the heavy presence of spacelane officers on high-altitude swoops, tempers flared as star cruisers and shuttle craft jockeyed for position outside the landing platforms.

Fourteen-year-old Anakin Skywalker swerved the Galan starfighter to avoid a cruiser trying to cut in the line waiting to land. "Watch it, you gravel-maggot!" he yelled, even though he knew the pilot couldn't hear him.

Beside him his Master, Obi-Wan Kenobi, cleared his throat.

"I know, I know," Anakin said. "Feel my anger, and let it go. But do I have to be a Jedi all the time, even in space traffic?" He flashed a grin at his Master. He knew the answer.

"You are a Jedi every moment," Obi-Wan said. "Even when another cruiser is sneaking in to your right."

"What?" Anakin wrenched his attention back to his piloting. A silver star cruiser was attempting to nose in — Anakin swerved to the left and then slid neatly into the empty slot ahead.

Obi-Wan leaned back in his seat. "If you allowed someone to cut in line, we would lose five minutes' time. Would that be so bad?"

His Master could always find an opportunity for a lesson, even while waiting to land in a crowded space-lane. "I guess not," Anakin said. "We're not in a hurry. But it's not right for them to try to sneak ahead of others."

"No," Obi-Wan said. "But that is the other pilot's choice. By trying to prevent him, you are feeding your own anger and impatience. Perhaps that is worse."

Anakin saw his Master's point. That was the trouble. Obi-Wan always made sense. The only problem was that Obi-Wan didn't understand how good it felt when Anakin had zoomed ahead, preventing the cruiser from cutting in.

The spacelane officer ahead signaled to Anakin. A new lane had opened up for landings. Anakin slid the craft neatly into place. Now that he was first in line, he could look around and enjoy the sight of so many star cruisers in one atmosphere.

"I knew it would be crowded on Euceron, but I didn't expect this," Anakin said. "At least on Coruscant the traffic is strictly controlled. This is a mess."

"Euceron isn't used to such traffic," Obi-Wan agreed. "Beings come from all over the galaxy to the Galactic Games."

"I didn't realize they would all arrive at once." Anakin wasn't really grumbling. He enjoyed the chaos, the scramble for lane space, the chance to see so many different kinds of star cruisers.

When he had first learned of the mission ahead, Anakin couldn't believe his luck. All he and his Master had to do was patrol the Galactic Games, keeping alert for any signs of trouble. The Galactic Games were held every seven years, and planets all over the galaxy competed to become the host planet. The Games were exciting and sometimes dangerous, with the fastest and most skilled competing in races and contests. Anakin couldn't wait to see the various events.

The government of Euceron had asked for Jedi help in order to keep the peace. In only seven years, the galaxy had changed. New trouble spots erupted far too often. Some systems had grievances with the Senate;

some planets had trade conflicts with other planets. Beings from many different worlds would be in close quarters, some of them hostile to one another. It could be a volatile mix.

Then again, everyone was coming to have a good time. Anakin knew that he was. The Galactic Games had been started over eight decades before in order to promote peace through sport. Winners became famous both on their own planets and in places they had never traveled. Even as a slave on Tatooine, Anakin had heard tales of their determination and mastery.

"Euceron is trying its best to keep things under control," Obi-Wan observed. "The leaders of the Ruling Power don't want anything to go wrong. They are trying to gain more power in the Senate, to be put on some very important committees. This is a crucial way to show that their planet is stable."

Anakin nodded, a bit bored by Senatorial politics. He was notified that he could land now on the Euceron City landing platform. A series of laser signals told him which slot to take. He came in fast and low, executing a quick turn that dropped the starfighter into position perfectly. He glanced over at his Master, knowing he had been a bit of a show-off, but Obi-Wan was already beginning arrival procedures.

Anakin reached for their survival packs and activated the landing ramp, which led to the greeting center high above the capital city, Eusebus. He couldn't wait to get going.

"This will be a good opportunity for you to reflect on a new Jedi lesson," Obi-Wan said. "Connection with the Living Force. There are beings from all over the galaxy here. You'll pick up many kinds of energies. With such a variety of beings crowded onto one planet, there is much to learn."

"Yes, Master." Anakin hovered by the doorway, waiting impatiently while Obi-Wan double-checked to make sure the cabin of their craft was secure. He made sure to keep his body still, however. He might not have conquered his agitation though he had learned to mask it.

But it was rare that his Master did not pick up on his feelings. Obi-Wan noted his impatience. "All right, young Padawan. Let's go."

Anakin walked out onto the landing ramp, his eyes eagerly sweeping the platform. Star pilots chatted in small groups, children dashed past parents' reaching fingers, air taxis unloaded passengers who lunged for their luggage — Wookiees and Babbs and everything in between. Everyone seemed in a terrific hurry to get somewhere. And the Games had not yet begun!

"Are you picking up anything about the mission ahead?" Obi-Wan asked him curiously. His Master often asked the question as soon as they stepped foot on a planet. Sometimes he even asked it before they landed, if he sensed that Anakin was swept by intuitions about the mission to come.

Anakin reached out to the Force. Sometimes it felt so easy. The Force was there, right within his grasp, and he could fold it around himself as easily as slipping into his travel cloak.

"I don't feel darkness here," he said. "I feel tremendous energy. It is not all good, but it isn't dark. It's just . . ."

"Life," Obi-Wan finished. "Emotion, expectation, hope, worry, excitement."

"It feels more intense," Anakin said slowly as they walked through the crowd.

"Because it is," Obi-Wan said. "We are all packed into one small city, waiting for a big event." He paused to consult a coordinates kiosk. "We will be staying in the official Games quarters, but let's explore a bit first."

They squeezed aboard a crowded turbolift that brought them down from the greeting center to the surface of the planet. They spilled out onto the main boulevard of Eusebus. The streets were crowded with speeders of every kind and description, and the many beings jostled and pushed their way to their destinations. Large overhead signs blinked out directions and

routes, such as STADIUM ONE: LEFT ON USIRINE STREET or STA-
DIUM TEN: TAKE AIR TRANSIT GREEN.

The aroma of the various food stands wafted toward them. Anakin's stomach growled. Meat sizzled on grills and sweets hung from slender poles that danced in the brisk wind, tantalizing him. He had eaten his morning meal only an hour before, but he suddenly felt hungry.

"Look around," Obi-Wan directed. "Tell me if you see anything out of the ordinary."

The ordinary? There didn't seem to be anything ordinary in Euceron City. It was a city built entirely of plastoid materials, since there was no native stone. The buildings were brightly colored and no higher than twenty stories. Eucerons were a humanoid species with large domed heads and delicate limbs. They dressed in neutral colors as if to offset their colorful structures.

But Obi-Wan had seen something Anakin should have noted. Anakin screened out his rapidly growing appetite and opened his mind to careful observation. It took him a few minutes, but then he felt it.

"There are security officers everywhere," he said. "They are not in uniform, but they are patrolling." He could tell they were security only by noting their watchful eyes constantly sweeping the crowd.

"Yes. Nicely observed, Padawan," Obi-Wan said. "Euceron has the largest security force in the galaxy for its size. The Ruling Power needs the security officers to keep the population under control. It is government by repression and intimidation. The Ruling Power is made up of ten rulers who make all laws and decisions. The city looks peaceful and prosperous, but the Ruling Power has been working for years to make it look that way. They are cultivating an image, and they are typically aggressive about their methods."

"So why should the Jedi help them?" Anakin wondered.

"The Ruling Power is not the kind of government the Senate would normally support," Obi-Wan agreed. "But the safety of many beings depends on the Games proceeding well, and that is important for the continued peace of the galaxy itself. So don't forget that this mission is a serious one. There are always beings in the galaxy who use these large gatherings for their own ends. Sabotage is always a possibility, so the Jedi are needed."

"Are we supposed to meet with the other Jedi teams?" Anakin asked. He hoped to see Tru Veld, a fellow Padawan and one of his few friends at the Temple.

"Yes. We'll need to coordinate our patrols," Obi-Wan said. "We'll see them at our quarters later."

Obi-Wan did not break his stride, but suddenly his concentration shifted. Anakin could see the change.

"Something is wrong," he murmured.

Anakin threw his own attention out like a net. He was aware of a change in the sound of the crowd. "A disturbance," he said.

"This way." Obi-Wan stepped up his pace. He threaded through the pedestrians.

Ahead was a large square. Food stalls were packed in tightly, and cafés ringed the edges.

Anakin saw a knot of beings across the square. They were packed so tightly it was difficult to see what they were looking at.

He heard a roar of anger. He did not know the language, but it was easy to guess the intent.

"Hurry." Obi-Wan tried to make it through the crowd, but the beings were crowded so densely now that it was impossible.

"Get out of my way or I'll kill you!" Someone shouted the words in Basic.

Now Anakin could see a Phlog, a giant being with a vibrosword, standing over a small Ortolan, a blue-furred creature armed with only a cup of juice. The Phlog waved the vibrosword close to his neighbor's nose. Instead of retreating, the crowd surged forward, interested in a possible fight.

"Go ahead, you tub of bantha fat," the Ortolan sneered.

"This isn't good," Obi-Wan muttered.

Suddenly the Phlog took his vibrosword and slashed through a small stone table. The group who had been sitting at it fell backward. One of them sprang up and withdrew a blaster. The giant Phlog grabbed both huge slabs of stone and lifted them over his head.

"I'll kill you all!"

Frustrated, Obi-Wan tried to get through the crowd. The beings had formed a solid wall of flesh and muscle. The Jedi could not move. But they weren't about to fail in their objective before the Games had even begun.

CHAPTER TWO

Anakin saw a sudden flash of blue. A lightsaber danced in the air and came down, slicing expertly through the thick slabs of stone. The movement was so fast that a tiny curl of smoke was the only evidence of the lightsaber's trail. The slabs dissolved into rocks and dust. The Phlog howled as one of the stone pieces fell on his foot.

"That should slow you down a minute."

Jedi Knight Siri's tone was pleasant, but it rang with the shimmer of durasteel. Next to her stood Ferus Olin, her Padawan. His lightsaber was raised and ready, his expression hard. He was prepared to spring if anyone moved, and everyone seemed to know it. A hush settled on the crowd.

The Phlog stood awkwardly, holding his foot. "Who are you?" he bellowed.

The Euceron whose table had been pulverized quickly shoved his blaster into his belt. "Ah, Jedi. Just defending myself," he muttered, backing away.

The Ortolan nodded rapidly, his blue fur flying. "Easy in such crowds to bump by accident."

"Exactly," Siri said. "So an apology is called for."

"Sorry," the Ortolan said quickly.

"By both of you," Siri said meaningfully, her gaze boring into Phlog, who towered several meters over her blond head.

The Phlog hesitated. He was not accustomed to apologizing for his temper. Even with a lightsaber centimeters from his neck.

For a moment, it seemed that the Phlog would launch an attack on Siri. She was ready.

By now Obi-Wan and Anakin had snaked through the crowd and were standing by, close enough to spring forward if needed. With a look, Obi-Wan told Anakin to hang back.

Ferus Olin stepped forward. "Think twice, my friend," he said in a soft tone. "Then think again."

Anakin saw the admiration on his Master's face at the coolness of Ferus's approach. A flare of jealousy rose inside him. Ferus always knew the right thing to say and the right way to say it. Ferus was only two years older than Anakin, but he was known for his maturity.

"Well, well, my fault," the Phlog said in false cheerfulness. "Let me buy you another juice."

He bent over the small Ortolan and led him into the café.

Siri deactivated her lightsaber. "There. Everyone is sorry. Incident over." Her clear voice sailed out over the crowd. "We can all get back to what we were doing."

The crowd that had been eager to witness a brawl suddenly melted away. Siri caught sight of Obi-Wan.

"Just a minute too late, as usual," she said.

"We were just waiting to see how you'd handle it," Obi-Wan answered. "I always wanted to see you go against a Phlog."

Anakin watched Obi-Wan and Siri. A stranger would never know that they were old friends.

He nodded a greeting at Ferus, who nodded stiffly back. There was no need to pretend that they liked each other. Ferus had warned him once that he did not trust him and would keep an eye on him. This had infuriated Anakin, and he still wasn't over it. He had let his anger go, but his resentment still simmered. He knew how a Jedi was supposed to handle that, but he couldn't.

He could not speak to Obi-Wan about it, either. He

didn't want his Master to know that a fellow Padawan, especially one as gifted and respected as Ferus, did not trust him.

He turned his attention back to Siri and Obi-Wan, who were talking in low voices.

". . . with the crowds like this," Obi-Wan was saying. "It was hard to get to you at all."

"And where was security?" Siri asked. "I saw officers all around undercover, but when they were needed, they were strangely absent."

"Perhaps fewer of them should be undercover," Obi-Wan suggested. "Some should be more visible."

Siri frowned. "The Eucerons hate the security forces. That's why they're undercover. But still, with so many visitors, keeping the peace is the first order of business."

"I'll talk to Liviani Sarno about it," Obi-Wan said, referring to the head of the Games Council.

Anakin couldn't believe it. Obi-Wan hadn't seen Siri in a while, and he only spoke of the mission! Anakin had great respect for Obi-Wan's wisdom, but sometimes he wondered how his Master could connect to the Living Force when his feelings were kept so tightly under wraps.

"Anakin!" Anakin heard the cheerful voice behind him and quickly turned. Tru Veld was loping across the plaza next to his Master, the tall and silent Ry-Gaul. Tru extended one long, flexible arm in a floppy wave that conveyed his excitement and happiness at seeing his friend. He and Tru had been in the same year of training at the Temple, but they had become friends after they had been chosen as Padawans.

Ry-Gaul nodded at Obi-Wan and Siri as they came up, but gave no verbal greeting. The three Masters huddled together for a discussion, leaving the three Padawans to talk among themselves.

"I can't decide, can you?" Tru asked Anakin, his eyes dancing. They were the color of the silver seas of Teevan, his home planet, and when he was excited they sparkled like sunlight on waves.

Anakin was used to Tru starting a conversation midway through. He lifted an eyebrow at him.

"Which Game events to attend," Tru explained. "They all sound fun."

"We are here to keep the peace," Ferus said. "Not to have fun."

Annoyance ran through Anakin. Ferus could spoil a good mood quicker than a double nova. Tru merely shook his head good-naturedly and nudged Ferus with a shoulder. "Relax, friend. I can keep the peace and watch the Games, too. Even our Masters will allow that."

"We haven't received our instructions," Ferus said.

"I am sure our instructions will be to avoid having a good time at all costs," Tru said to Ferus in a mock-serious tone, his eyes still twinkling with silent amusement.

Ferus sighed. "Padawans are always trying to get me to relax," he said. "I'm just not made that way."

Siri, Ry-Gaul, and Obi-Wan turned away from their conference and approached their Padawans.

"We've decided that you three can go off on your own for a while," Obi-Wan told them. "But be sure your comlinks are functioning at all times."

Anakin and Tru exchanged an excited glance. They hadn't expected this good fortune. They had hoped to run into each other, but now they could actually attend at least some of the Games together! Anakin would even put up with Ferus if it meant he could spend time with Tru.

"I contacted Liviani Sarno. She's on her way here," Obi-Wan told them. "After we receive a briefing, you'll be free to go. Then we'll all meet back at the Games quarters for the evening meal."

Within moments they saw a tall female Euceron heading toward them. She was dressed in a scarlet robe embroidered with orange and gold threads, and her crown of braids was woven with bright jewels. Liviani Sarno was not hard to spot.

Traveling in her wake were three other beings, and Anakin was surprised that he knew two of them. He had met Didi and Astri when they still owned the Coruscant café that Dexter Jettster now ran. He knew that they had been close to Qui-Gon Jinn and were friends with Obi-Wan as well.

Didi's round brown eyes widened when he saw Obi-Wan. Astri ran forward, her pretty face flushed.

"Obi-Wan!" Dark curls flying, Astri threw herself at Obi-Wan, wrapping her arms around him. Anakin was surprised to see his reserved Master break out into a huge smile and hug Astri back. Didi came up and tried to hug both of them, but his plump arms were too short. He settled for thumping Obi-Wan on the back.

"This makes my eyes new and my heart glad!" Didi cried.

"It is so good to see you!" Astri exclaimed.

"It is good to see you, too," Obi-Wan said. "You are here to see the Games?"

"In an official capacity," Astri said. "I'd like you to meet my husband, Bog Divinian. He's on the Games Council. Bog, this is the great Jedi Knight, Obi-Wan Kenobi."

Bog Divinian was a tall, handsome man in a plumfruit-colored tunic almost as bright as Liviani Sarno's.

"I am honored to meet a Jedi," Bog said. "Do you know Liviani Sarno?"

"This is our first meeting," Obi-Wan said with a quick nod. He introduced the Padawans. Siri coolly assessed the Council member. Ry-Gaul stood silent.

"We are glad the Jedi accepted the request of the Ruling Power to monitor the Games," Liviani said. "We can use the help. Many more came than we expected."

"We have to keep things running smoothly," Bog added. "Liviani is doing an amazing job of organization."

Liviani inclined her head in the fashion of one who is used to compliments.

"If you need an insider's perspective, I'll be glad to help," Bog added, speaking to Obi-Wan. "Because you're such a good friend of Astri's, I'll make time for you."

Obi-Wan's polite expression did not falter, but Siri's ice-blue eyes flashed at the notion that Bog would only help the Jedi because one of them was a personal friend. Ry-Gaul just blinked impassively.

"Thank you," Obi-Wan said smoothly. No doubt he had noticed Astri's embarrassment.

"Obi-Wan Kenobi is the greatest of all Jedi Knights," Didi said proudly. "He will not need our help, I guarantee." He suddenly realized that he had insulted Siri and Ry-Gaul and turned to them quickly. "Not that Siri and Ry-Gaul aren't equally great. All Jedi are great!" Didi beamed at all of them. "Even Padawans!"

"How are the preparations going?" Obi-Wan asked Liviani. "Any problems?"

"So smoothly, no problems," Bog Divinian answered. "The Games Council is handling everything beautifully. Maxo Vista is a native of Euceron and on the Council, and he has been very helpful. You know of him, of course."

Obi-Wan shook his head politely. Anakin couldn't believe his Master didn't know the great Euceron hero who had stunned the galaxy seven years before by winning five events at the Galactic Games on Berrun.

"But everyone knows Maxo Vista!" Bog said, surprised. "He is renowned throughout the galaxy! He might not be wealthy, but he *is* famous. And he is a good friend of mine, so if you need an introduction . . ."

Siri snorted, then tried to turn it into a cough. Anakin remembered that Obi-Wan had told him that Siri had never done very well in her diplomacy classes at the Temple.

Even Didi looked embarrassed at Bog's bragging. He smiled at the Jedi in turn. "Who needs galactic heroes when we have Jedi?"

"Precisely," Liviani said crisply. "And Bog is wrong about our not having problems."

Bog looked crestfallen at having disappointed Liviani. "I know of no problems, Liviani."

Liviani ignored Bog and turned to the Jedi. "There are rumors that there will be an illegal Podrace on the outskirts of the city."

Anakin suddenly became very interested.

Siri frowned. "We had not heard this."

Liviani nodded. "Podracers from all over the galaxy have been spotted arriving on Euceron. We have heard that they are gathering on the city's northern border in the Great Dordon Caves, whose extensive tunnels are, unfortunately, ideally suited for this suicidal sport."

"Podracing is illegal in the Core Worlds," Bog said disapprovingly. "If I were Senator — I am running for Senator of my home planet of Nuralee, by the way — I would consider introducing a law to outlaw Podracing galaxy-wide. It only promotes gambling and violence." Bog gave a quick glance at Liviani to see if she approved of his declaration.

Liviani continued to ignore him, however. "You see our problem," she said to the Jedi. "The Ruling Power is worried about bad publicity, so it wants us to ignore the rumors. If Podracers die in the caves, no one will care, officially." Liviani's delicate eyebrows drew together in a worried frown. "But the authorities underestimate how popular these races are. Beings will hear of them. Betting will take place, and spectators — some of them quite important on their home planets — will find the race. We cannot guarantee safety and crowd control."

"The Games must proceed smoothly," Bog added. "Absolutely."

Anakin barely heard their voices. His brain had started to buzz as soon as he'd heard the word *Pod race.* He hadn't seen or been in one since he was a slave on Tatooine.

It was as though the thick clouds overhead parted, for suddenly he felt the blow of the hot suns of Tatooine on the back of his neck. He could taste the grit of sand between his teeth. And he could feel the rise of the same fierce desire that had filled him as a young boy, the simplest, most powerful feeling he knew: the will to win.

Anakin felt his Master's eyes on him, as though the surge of feeling had touched Obi-Wan like a warning finger. A mask of serenity dropped over Anakin's face. He could call it up at will for times such as this, times when his blood seemed to race closer to his skin.

Liviani was speaking, and Obi-Wan turned back to her. Anakin kept his expression calm but interested. Like a Jedi would be. But inside . . . inside he was a slave boy, on fire to race again.

CHAPTER THREE

Does he really think he's fooling me?

Obi-Wan's exasperation with his Padawan did not show on his face. Anakin's attempts to hide his excitement may have tricked the others, but Obi-Wan felt it charge the air. He had never seen Anakin compete in a Podrace, and Qui-Gon had not given him many details, but he knew how outrageously dangerous Podracing was. Pilots sat in open cockpits, racing fragile crafts that were powered by massive engines tethered to the racer by flexible cables. Obi-Wan could imagine that the prospect of Anakin once again pitting his skills and reflexes and daring in such a race would be irresistible.

But it would not be worthy of a Jedi. Jedi did not seek thrills.

Obi-Wan could understand a momentary tug toward

the past. He would expect his Padawan to overcome it. A longing for such things was childish, in his opinion. As soon as they were alone, he would speak to Anakin about it. . . .

"Obi-Wan, my friend?" Didi spoke in a low tone at his elbow. "A word?"

Liviani had received a call on her comlink and had turned away, so Obi-Wan followed Didi a few paces away from the others.

"I just wanted to say," Didi began, smoothing his tunic with plump fingers, "how my entire being is convulsed with joy to see your handsome and noble face once again —"

"You want a favor," Obi-Wan said flatly. He was fond of Didi, but he did not for one second think that Didi would hesitate to take advantage of their friendship.

Didi looked wounded. "Not a favor. Some company on a little errand —"

Obi-Wan began to turn away in dismissal.

"All right, all right! The truth! A favor!" Didi said quickly. He spread his hands, palms out. "But such a tiny one it hardly qualifies."

Obi-Wan closed his eyes for a second in irritation. *Qui-Gon would ask for my patience.* "What is it?"

"Shortly after arriving in Eusebus, I bought a swoop bike," Didi said. "I thought it would make navigating these crowded streets much easier. However, hardly had I gone two meters when the engine . . . whoosh, ka-blam!" Didi's fingers traced an explosion in the air. "I want my money back, yet I fear that slimy son of a monkey-lizard will refuse me."

"But not if a Jedi is along," Obi-Wan said wearily.

"You would not have to do a thing! Just stand there and look invincible. Maybe casually take your lightsaber out and test it . . ."

"No. No lightsaber."

"Then your presence only." Didi put his hands together. "Such a big favor it would be, and I would repay it a thousand times over."

"Do you really think," Obi-Wan said, exasperated, "that I have time to help you make up a bad deal?"

"Of course not, you are so busy being strong and good," Didi said. "But while we are together, I can give you a behind-the-scenes, sneak-peek look at the Games. Bog is my son-in-law and on the Council. I have a unique perspective." Didi could see that Obi-Wan was unmoved. "Now, don't do it for Qui-Gon's sake. I would never want you to remember how much he loved me and how many times he helped me. Don't even mention his beloved name!"

"I don't have to," Obi-Wan said. "You just did." But he knew from the first moment that Didi had drawn him aside that he would help him. The truth was that Obi-Wan had a soft spot for Didi just as vulnerable as Qui-Gon's had been. And he had come to see that it wasn't such a bad thing, to feel affection for a worthless scoundrel with a big heart.

Still, there were limits.

"I will give you ten minutes," Obi-Wan said.

"You are the best and kindest friend I ever —"

"Nine minutes, fifty-seven seconds —"

Didi's mouth snapped shut. "I will tell Astri. One moment."

Didi dashed off, and Siri came up next to Obi-Wan. "You are worse than Qui-Gon," she said in an amused tone.

Obi-Wan shrugged. "I am still his Padawan in many ways."

"Ry-Gaul and I are going with Liviani. She has some swoops available for us so we can get an overview of the area. We're sending the Padawans off on their own. The opening rituals will begin in a few minutes."

"I'll keep in touch and meet up with you," Obi-Wan said. "This won't take long."

Siri cocked her head. Her hands slid into the pockets of the unisuit she wore instead of a tunic. "The amazing thing is that you actually believe that," she said.

CHAPTER FOUR

When Anakin had first seen Tru, he had immediately wanted to spend time with him. Now he could hardly wait to leave him behind. This wasn't Tru's fault — Anakin just wanted time alone to explore. About Podracing.

He walked alongside Ferus and Tru. The streets were crowded and they had trouble staying together. Ferus didn't seem to notice. He strode ahead at the pace he always set, talking without making sure the others were able to hear.

"The opening rituals are at Stadium One," Ferus said. "We could take an air taxi, but there don't seem to be many around."

"We can get there on Transit Yellow," Tru said. "Four

stops. I memorized the transit system maps on the way here."

"It's the perfect opportunity for us to see all sorts of beings from all over the galaxy," Ferus said. "We should observe customs and protocol."

Leave it to Ferus to have a lesson plan for the afternoon, Anakin thought.

As if he had read Anakin's thoughts and was afraid he would speak them aloud, Tru extended one flexible arm and slid his hand over Anakin's mouth.

Anakin batted it away with a grin. No doubt Tru was remembering their mission to the planet Radnor, when Anakin and Ferus had argued every step of the way. But Anakin had no desire to argue with Ferus again. He didn't care about him enough to argue.

He had more important things to do — like check out the Podracers. Anakin told himself that someone on the Jedi teams needed to do so. Logically, he was the best candidate. He was the only one who had raced, and he was sure to know some of the beings involved. He hadn't raced since he was eight years old, six and a half years ago. But the racers tended to keep racing, if they weren't killed.

Of course, Obi-Wan hadn't asked him to check out the Podracers. But he had left him free to choose what he wanted to see. Anakin assured himself that he wasn't disobeying Obi-Wan by going.

Still, he didn't want to advertise his plans to his fellow Padawans. He could trust Tru, but Ferus was another matter. It would be just like Ferus to make a big deal of it.

"I'll catch up with you later," he told Ferus and Tru. "I have something I need to check out first."

Disappointment clouded Tru's silvery eyes. "Oh?"

Anakin knew that Tru had been looking forward to spending time with him, too. When you made friends among the Jedi, you treasured the times you were together because they could be rare.

Ferus gave him a glance that was more pointed. "Obi-Wan asked you to do something?"

Anakin could not lie. Not even to Ferus. He pretended he had not heard him over the noise of the crowd. He turned to go, and Tru leaned over and spoke softly in his ear. "Transit Red, end of the line."

So Tru did know where he was headed.

"You're a good friend," Anakin said as he dashed off before Ferus could say anything more.

Eusebus had converted its largest air taxis to a free transit system. He found Transit Red and hopped aboard. He didn't mind missing the opening rituals, which no doubt would be filled with parading teams and boring speeches. The real fun was taking place else-where.

At the last stop on Transit Red, the buildings ended abruptly. There was no gradual thinning of structures. An apartment block ended, the road narrowed, and the horizon was before him. There appeared to be nothing in sight but bare hills.

Now what? Anakin wondered as he descended from the air taxi and looked from right to left.

He closed his eyes and summoned the Force. He felt it rise from the red dust and bound off the hills back at him. And then he felt the Living Force as a wave that gathered momentum and broke over him in a shower of light.

There.

He took off toward the hills to his left. Well, if this mission was supposed to teach him about the Living Force, he doubted there was much to learn. Sometimes he thought he was in better touch with the Living Force than his Master. Obi-Wan lived in his head. His emotions were reserved. Anakin often had no idea what his Master felt or thought. Sometimes he seemed to respond to the beings they met on their travels simply as ways to get something accomplished. A scrappy pilot with hair-raising stories of smuggling tech parts through the Outer Rim systems was just a means to get from the Manda spaceport to Circarpous Major. A tavern owner who kept pet dinkos was a contact to discover the location of a possible weapons cache. A young brother and sister bounty-hunting team was taken along just to provide an answer to the mystery of who was behind a Jedi's kidnapping.

It wasn't that Obi-Wan lacked compassion, Anakin mused. It was just that there was a little more distance between him and other living beings. Qui-Gon had not been able to pass along his connection to the Living Force to his Padawan, Anakin felt.

Anakin treasured his Master. But sometimes he wondered what it would have been like to have Qui-Gon as a Master instead. Would Qui-Gon have shared his feelings more easily? Anakin had felt a connection to Qui-Gon from the start. It had taken more time with Obi-Wan. It was still taking time.

He reached the hills, which were covered with thorny green bushes and small, squat trees. Anakin followed the hillside until he spotted scorch marks, then an abandoned hydrospanner. He was close.

He strode forward ten meters, pushed aside a dense covering of leaves, and found the cave opening. He walked inside, already feeling the presence of living beings. The cave opened out as he walked. There were two security guards, but they were unaware of Anakin's silent tread. Soon the ceiling soared a hundred meters over his head.

He heard the clang of metal. The muffled sound of shouts and curses. The whine and sputter of engines being tuned and tweaked. The roar of powerful turbines. Someone whistling off-tune and someone else shouting at him to stop or he'd shove an oily rag down his slimy throat.

Anakin smiled. It sounded like home.

The cave opened out and he saw a makeshift pit hangar set up ahead. Podracers were parked haphazardly while beings of every size and description and varying degrees of oil-soaked clothing worked on them. Pit droids scuttled about, hauling huge lubricant hoses and tugging power cell chargers.

He stopped at the edge and watched for a moment. Hydrospanners clanged and macrofusers flew. Someone yelled for a fusioncutter. Some of the Podracer pilots sat on elaborate folding chairs, sipping grog or tea and keeping a watchful eye on their mechanics. Other pilots, not yet rich enough to have someone else to tweak their engines, worked steadily and with enormous concentration. The smallest mistake could cause a Podracer to turn a fraction too sluggishly, resulting in a spectacular crash.

Anakin recognized Aldar Beedo, a Glymphid he had

raced against several times. He was surprised Beedo was still alive, let alone racing. Beedo had never been particularly skillful, but he'd been cunning and fearless and willing to cheat, and that had made him more successful at Podracing than he had any right to be. Anakin would have thought he'd have crashed or been run out of the Podraces by this time. Then again, there wasn't much policing of Podracing. Race officials attempted to keep some sort of control, but Podracers schemed to get away with as much as they could.

Anakin noticed a Podracer mechanic nearby. He could only see a pair of short legs sticking out from underneath while another mechanic stood near the console, pushing buttons in what appeared to be a random fashion. The two mechanics were Aleenas. He recognized their three-toed feet and bluish scaly skin. The Podracer looked familiar. It had been re-painted and buffed, but he was sure he recognized it. He took a couple of steps closer.

"Doby, hand me that hydrospanner, will you? I've almost got this fused. Then we can start her up again."

A hydrospanner twirled through the air, nearly taking off the tip of Anakin's nose. A hand reached up from underneath the Podracer and caught it.

"Go ahead and use it, but I'm telling you, Deland,

it's not the joint," the mechanic at the console said. "No chance, never ever. If the engine overheats during gear switches, it's got to be a sensor problem."

"But the sensor doesn't show a problem, blope-head."

"That's the problem, bantha-breath. If you'd just let me finish checking out the sensor suite . . ."

"I've been doing this longer than you have, baby brother, so slap your flapping lips shut."

"You're only fourteen months older . . ."

"Fourteen and a half. And I'm the pilot. You're the mechanic."

"My point exact —"

"Got it!" A face stained with grease appeared in a pair of grimy welding goggles. Deland sprang to his feet in one motion. "Let's fire her up."

"I wouldn't do that if I were you," Anakin said.

Doby and Deland peered at him from behind their goggles.

"And we should listen to you because?" Deland asked.

Anakin took a step closer. "Because if your engine is overheating during gear changes, the problem could be in the current filter. Have you used an impulse detector?" The words flowed easily, like a native language he had not spoken in years but would never forget.

"Not that it's your business, but yes," Doby said. "It didn't show anything wrong."

"Then it's definitely the current filter," Anakin said. "It's clogged."

"Slap it shut, you son of a durkii," Deland warned his brother. "This guy could be working for another Pod-racer. He's just trying to spook us."

Doby leaned toward his brother and said in a whisper, "Haven't you noticed? He's a Jedi."

"He's a fraud and a fake," Deland hissed. "Sebulba probably hired him."

Anakin felt a rush of heat that made his face flame. Back on Tatooine, Sebulba the Dug had tried to cheat his way to victory in the Boonta Eve race and nearly killed Anakin in the process. They had always sparred, though Sebulba had never taken him seriously enough to worry about him. Until the race on Boonta Eve, when he'd beaten him in an extremely close race. "Sebulba is still racing?"

"Everybody knows that," Deland said. "Now I know you're lying. Doby, fire up that engine!"

"You're going to blow out the intake valves on the turbines," Anakin warned.

In answer, Deland reached over and flipped on the engine. Anakin had already stepped out of the way. A loud explosion blew Deland back onto the ground. Doby was almost blasted by a roar of fire from the left turbine. Anakin reached over and shut off the engine.

"I'll be a Kowakian monkey-lizard!" Doby cried. "You were right!"

Deland picked himself up and dusted off his leggings. "Lucky guess."

"Are you two related to Ratts Tyerell?" Anakin asked curiously. "I think I recognize this Podracer."

Doby nodded proudly. "He was our father. He died in the great Boonta Eve Classic six years ago. Did you know him?"

"I raced against him in that race," Anakin said. "He was one of the fastest. Incredibly quick reflexes."

"Not quick enough," Doby said sorrowfully.

"Lying again," Deland said to Anakin. "No human can be a Podracer."

"One was," Doby said. "A human child. A slave. He won his freedom, and after the race he disappeared. His name was —"

"Anakin Skywalker," Anakin supplied. "Pleased to meet you."

"Now you're a Jedi?" Doby asked in disbelief. "And you were a slave?"

"It's a strange galaxy," Anakin said with a grin.

"Totally true," Doby agreed.

"Don't want to interrupt this getting-to-know-you gush, but we have a job to do," Deland said gruffly.

"I'll help you if you want," Anakin said spontaneously. He'd love to get his hands on a Podracer engine again, but he knew Obi-Wan would certainly disapprove.

"What's in it for you?" Deland asked suspiciously.

"Who cares?" Doby asked. "He beat Sebulba, Deland! Now we have to." He turned to Anakin. "After our father died, we had no money, so our uncle sold our sister into slavery. Djulla's master is now Sebulba. We have to get her out of his clutches! We bet our Podracer that we'd win. Sebulba bet Djulla's freedom. This time, though, he's not racing. His son Hekula is."

"I'm sorry that your sister is a slave," Anakin said. "Do you know Shmi, my mother? She's a slave, too. Or she was, when I saw her last."

Doby shook his head. "Mos Espa is full of beings. We don't know them all."

Anakin blinked as tears filled his eyes, surprising him. For a moment, Shmi had seemed so close. But she was as far away as she always was. He turned away quickly, his gaze roaming around the makeshift hangar. He didn't see Sebulba. But he did see something familiar — his old Podracer. Could it be?

"Whose Podracer is that?" he asked, pointing it out.

"Hekula's," Deland said, giving it a glance.

Yes, it was definitely Anakin's old Podracer, a customized Radon-Ulzer. It had been painted and retooled, but he would recognize it anywhere. He knew Qui-Gon had sold the Podracer, but not to whom. Sebulba must have bought it. Anakin burned at the thought of Sebulba owning the Podracer he had built and maintained so lovingly.

A tall young Dug suddenly moved into Anakin's field of vision. "What are you looking at, spy?" he shouted.

"What I look at is not your concern," Anakin shot back.

"When it's my Podracer it is," the Dug hissed back. "Spy!"

"It's Hekula," Doby warned Anakin in a whisper. "Be careful."

Anakin looked at Sebulba's son carefully. He felt the dark side of the Force shimmer off him. He had taken after his father, that was clear.

A movement caught his eye. Another Dug had scuttled across the distance toward him.

Anakin found himself face-to-face with his old enemy, Sebulba.

CHAPTER FIVE

Anakin's fingers itched for his lightsaber. The last time Sebulba had threatened him, he'd been just a child and untrained. Now he could dispatch Sebulba before the Dug could manage to blink.

But he saw immediately that Sebulba didn't recognize him. His gaze was hostile, but the hostility wasn't personal. He had no idea that Anakin was the young slave boy who had humiliated him in a race years before.

Anakin smiled again.

The smile infuriated Sebulba. "What are you smiling at? And how dare you bully my son!"

"He's wasn't bullying me, Father," Hekula whined in Huttese. "I am bullying him!"

"You were doing a very poor job of it," Anakin answered in Huttese. "But that doesn't surprise me."

"How dare you!" Sebulba roared. "Prepare to die!"

Deland quickly moved between them. "Who's talking about dying?" he said in a jovial tone. "Let's save that for the Podrace. Right, Hekula? I'd worry about crashing more than spies, if I were you. I've seen you race!"

Hekula's long head thrust toward Deland. "You'll choke on my dust, son of a Ratt!"

Sebulba was more clever than his son. He grinned craftily and shot a look at Djulla, who was standing by Hekula's Podracer, preparing a snack for the two Dugs. "I hope you're alive to see your sister wipe the floor under our feet," he hissed. "For the next fifty years!"

Anakin and Deland both tensed, ready to strike. In Sebulba's taunt Anakin heard every cruelty he and his mother had ever endured.

Doby grabbed the hems of Anakin's and Deland's tunics. "Just let them go," he murmured. "We'll win the race. That is our better best revenge."

Anakin saw Deland's hand clench and unclench. His own fingertips burned to slip his lightsaber from its sheath.

"Let's leave the cowards to their play," Sebulba

sneered. He and Hekula slithered off, their footfalls clattering on the stony ground.

Deland wiped his oily hands with a rag viciously, as though wiping away the memory of Sebulba's taunt. "We've got to beat them. We've got to."

"He's fast," Doby said, watching Hekula and Sebulba return to their entourage. A look of pain crossed his face as Djulla handed Hekula a cup of juma juice and Hekula spat it out while shouting an insult. "He's just as cruel and dangerous as his father. Maybe more so, because he takes more chances."

Temptation loomed before Anakin. He could help Doby and Deland beat Hekula. He knew it. It was not part of his mission here. But Obi-Wan had allowed him to have free time. What better way to use it than free a slave from the grip of a harsh master?

"Sebulba taught him how to cheat, too," Deland said worriedly. "Come on, Doby. Let's get back to work."

"You can beat him." The certainty in Anakin's voice made the two brothers turn to face him. "With my help. Hekula has my old Podracer. I built it with my own hands. They may have painted it and buffed it, but I still know those engines. I know its weaknesses. I know how Sebulba cheats. I can help you win."

Doby and Deland exchanged a glance. "We can't ask you to do that," Deland said.

"You're not asking."

"We can't pay you," Doby said. "All of our credits are tied up in the Podracer. We barely have enough to get home."

"I don't need credits. And I don't need thanks," Anakin said. "I just need you to win."

CHAPTER SIX

"So you promised me inside information," Obi-Wan said to Didi. They could not locate an air taxi, and all the Transits were full, so they had to walk to the swoop seller. Obi-Wan didn't mind. It gave him a chance to get a feeling of the streets. He reached out to the Force and received nothing alarming back.

"My son-in-law is an idiot."

"That's not exactly the kind of information I had in mind," Obi-Wan said mildly.

Didi sighed. "You'd think Astri would have more sense. Did I raise her to fall for the first tall, handsome idiot who walked through my door? I did not! Is it my fault she picked such a stiff-necked, rule-following, small-spirited, mid-Rim, mid-minded, puffed-up bonehead?"

"Well, at least he's not a criminal," Obi-Wan said.

"Maybe Astri wanted a quieter life. Maybe she was tired of dealing with a rule-breaking, truth-stretching, scam-running scoundrel of a father."

"So it *is* my fault," Didi sniffed.

"Astri has always made her own choices, Didi. And they are hers to make. Now, you said you had insider news on the Games."

"Bog thinks that by serving on the Council for the Games, he'll get the backing of some important beings in the Senate, and that he'll be assigned important committee assignments. All he does is talk, talk, talk about how important his role is and what it will mean for his future." Didi mimicked a snore. "Honestly, I don't know how Astri stands it. His big job has been arranging the seating for some big-shot Senators. Hoo-diggety-hoo."

"Didi, you said you had *information*," Obi-Wan said. "This is *complaining*."

"I have plenty of information," Didi said. "How can I not? Bog never stops talking. But he never says anything worth listening to. Oh, look, here we are." Didi paused in front of a shop with closed durasteel shutters.

"It doesn't look open," Obi-Wan observed.

"Oh, it is. The seller just doesn't want to attract too many customers."

"Really. That doesn't sound typical."

"It's a very exclusive shop." Didi turned to him. "Remember, you don't have to say anything. Just stand there and give that Jedi-ish look."

"I think I can manage it," Obi-Wan said dryly. "Tell me something, Didi. If you want to return a swoop, shouldn't you have brought it with you?"

"I can fetch it in moments. No need to worry."

Didi rapped a rhythmic knock on the door. Several seconds later the door slid open. Obi-Wan realized that the pause of the few seconds meant that they had just undergone some sort of security check. Was the shopowner concerned about vandalism or theft? It was possible, since Eusebus was crowded with strangers.

But the security measures seemed excessive for a swoop seller. Obi-Wan stepped into the dim interior, fully aware that Didi could be leading him into his usual swamp of deception. Didi didn't so much lie as leave crucial pieces of information out.

You owe me one, Qui-Gon.

"Good afternoon, good afternoon," Didi said to a massive creature who suddenly loomed out of the shadows in the shop. The being was two meters taller than Obi-Wan. Each fifteen-fingered hand was the size of a bantha haunch.

There were six swoops parked in a random fashion

around the open space. There were no other customers and no sign of business that Obi-Wan could see.

"You may remember me," Didi said. "Didi Oddo. I was in yesterday."

The massive creature said nothing, just watched Didi with flat eyes.

"Then again, you may not," Didi said nervously. "This is my very good friend, the great Jedi Knight, Obi-Wan Kenobi. Obi-Wan, this is the swoop seller, Uso Yso."

The creature did not shift his gaze from Didi's face.

"Obviously you are a creature of action and I should get right to the point," Didi said. "The swoop I bought yesterday . . . I have changed my mind."

A flicker of alertness lit Uso Yso's opaque gaze.

"I would like my money back," Didi said, trying to sound forceful. "The swoop is not . . . not what I expected. No doubt I will return another day to buy a . . . different swoop, but not this one."

Finally, Uso Yso spoke. "No."

Didi took a delicate step backward. "One moment."

He leaned back and whispered to Obi-Wan. "Can't you draw your lightsaber or Jedi-move something? You don't have to kill him."

"No," Obi-Wan said.

"A deal is a deal," Uso Yso said, crossing his huge

arms. "You are insulting me with your presence. I do not like to be insulted."

"Ah, no insult intended. None at all," Didi said rapidly. "Just a polite request. Surely there beats a heart underneath that . . . ah, magnificent physique."

"Two hearts, actually," Uso Yso said. He withdrew an electro-jabber from his belt. "Would you like to continue the argument?"

Didi froze, staring at the weapon. He took another step back. "No argument. Just a thought. Such a pleasant afternoon. We must be going."

Didi almost ran from the shop. Obi-Wan followed. The door slid shut behind them, and Obi-Wan turned to Didi disgustedly.

"That was no swoop seller," he accused him.

"An unusual type, yes," Didi said. "Most helpful. Well, it's been such an unexpected pleasurable experience to see you, my friend, but I must be going —"

Obi-Wan stepped into his path. "Explain."

"Most happy to oblige, Obi-Wan," Didi said. "It is possible that the swoop seller might have an additional business."

"Ah," Obi-Wan said.

"Perhaps he sells swoops — I am sure he does, in fact, a few here and there — but that was not my business with him," Didi said evasively. His eyes darted about as if trying to find an escape route.

"Your business with him was?" Obi-Wan asked.

"A small bet," Didi said. He held up his hands as Obi-Wan glowered at him. "Such a tiny bet! On one of the events. Even the Jedi must realize that such an opportunity exists here on Euceron and there will be many who wish to place a wager."

"Certainly we realize that," Obi-Wan said. "It is also illegal. The Senate has banned gambling on the Galactic Games, and for good reason. It attracts criminals." He underlined the last word, giving Didi a sharp glance.

Didi nodded, frowning. "True. It would attract the wrong sort. Unlike me, who only places a bet now and again for the fun of it."

Obi-Wan sighed. "So why did you try to get your money back?"

"I was too impulsive," Didi confessed. "One of my faults, along with my generosity, that gets me into trouble. I made a wager and then my guilt overwhelmed me."

"Since when have you felt guilty about breaking the law?"

"I prefer to think I bend it, Obi-Wan. But that's not what caused my great guilt. It is because the credits I used were not mine."

"Whose were they?" Obi-Wan sensed he was nearing the real story at last.

"Bog and Astri's." Didi hung his head. "It was wrong. You cannot reproach me more than I have reproached myself. But they have a little wealth hidden away for some land Bog wishes to purchase, and this purchase will not be made for some time. The credits were just lying there! Such a waste. I assumed I could take the credits, make the bet, collect my winnings, and return the credits I borrowed without Astri knowing."

"And what if you lost?"

"I had such a sure tip, I did not think it possible."

Obi-Wan tapped a finger on his belt. Drawing information out of Didi was like trying to siphon water from sand. "If it is such a sure thing, why do you want your money back?"

"My guilt happened!" Didi said, his brown eyes wide. "I can't do that to Astri."

"And you also discovered that Bog and Astri would need the credits sooner than you thought," Obi-Wan guessed.

"Well, they happened to meet the owner of the land they want to buy here at the Games, and he is willing to sell at last . . ."

"So they will find the credits missing." Obi-Wan sighed. "There is only one thing to do. Confess what you've done to Astri. She will forgive you. She always does."

"Yes, doesn't she? That is a good idea, my friend. That is exactly what I will do."

Obi-Wan knew perfectly well that Didi would do nothing of the kind. "And do not involve me any further in your schemes," he said sternly. "You are on your own from now on. You cannot use the Jedi Order to threaten others."

"Not I!" Didi exclaimed in a hurt tone. "How can you say this, when I am the biggest supporter of Jedi in the galaxy? I did give you insider information, after all," he pointed out. "You now know the most important bookie at the Games."

"Am I supposed to thank you now?" Obi-Wan asked incredulously.

"No, no, of course not. Thanks is never what I want."

"Thanks are never what you deserve," Obi-Wan murmured.

"Ah, you joke." Didi smiled. "Then you are not angry with me. What a noble being you are, Obi-Wan Kenobi! How lucky I am to have you as a friend!"

"Not for much longer, if you try this again," Obi-Wan said. "Now I've wasted enough time. I must do my duty."

"Of course. Vastly more important than my humble problems. Do not worry about me. I will be fine," Didi said bravely.

Shaking his head, Obi-Wan left Didi, no doubt to concoct further schemes to get himself out of trouble. The gleam in Didi's eyes told him that.

Which reminded him of his Padawan. The gleam in Anakin's eyes had clearly told Obi-Wan that his Padawan would not be able to resist the lure of Podracing for long.

No doubt he was there now. After checking in with Siri and Ry-Gaul, Obi-Wan squeezed aboard a crowded Transit Red. By the time it reached the northern edge of the city he was the only one aboard. He jumped out and it turned around to speed back to the city. Obi-Wan stood in the center of a dusty road. Hills shimmered in the distance. He saw no sign of living beings.

He summoned the Force. As clearly as a directional laser, the Force told him where the cave entrance would be.

He struck off toward the hillside and climbed until he found a screen of thick green foliage. He pushed the bushes aside and found the cave entrance. Obi-Wan hiked inside. The coolness of the air felt good on his warm skin.

He found the pit hangar easily. His Padawan stood

over an engine, a hydrospanner in his hand. Obi-Wan came up behind him. Anakin was so absorbed that his usual sensitivity to his Master's presence was absent.

"It's got to be calibrated exactly right," Anakin was saying to two young Aleena mechanics standing nearby. "We might have to do it fifty times to get it right. Or we might get lucky and get it right in two."

"I hope it's the latter," Obi-Wan said. "Because there is a mission you should be attending to."

Anakin stood up so abruptly that he banged his head on the turbine. "Master! I didn't see you."

Obi-Wan examined the Podracer. "I see that you're busy."

"I thought I'd lend a hand to Doby and Deland. They're from Tatooine." Anakin looked uncomfortable. "If they win, they free their sister. She's a slave."

"I see." Obi-Wan nodded at the two brothers. "I wish you good luck. Anakin, may I speak with you a moment?"

He drew Anakin aside. "You know this is wrong," he told his Padawan with a frown. "I'm sure you are helping for the right reasons. But this is not our mission. We have more important things to do. And may I remind you that Podracing is illegal?"

"But the Ruling Power is looking the other way —"

"But the Games Council is concerned. As should

you be. Once word gets out, spectators will arrive. This could turn into a dangerous situation. Do you know what the course will be?"

"Through the caves," Anakin said excitedly. "Can you imagine the difficulties? And they've already thought about the spectators. They're going to set up a viewing stand near the finish line."

"That doesn't mean that they will be safe." Obi-Wan's comlink signaled, and he answered it brusquely.

The unfamiliar voice was frantic with urgency. "There is an emergency —"

"Who is this?" Obi-Wan asked.

"Bog. It's Bog. You must come immediately. The Official Quarters."

"What is wrong?"

"Come now!" Bog shouted, and the line went dead.

CHAPTER SEVEN

"We need transport," Obi-Wan said to Anakin.

Doby approached them. "We have an airspeeder," he said. "You are welcome to borrow it for as long as you need it. Anakin has helped us with no thought for himself, and we wish to repay him however we can."

"Thank you," Obi-Wan said. Although he was irritated with Anakin for heading straight to the Podraces, he was always glad to see how Anakin's generosity endeared him to others. Strangers became friends quickly for his Padawan.

Anakin connected to the Living Force as Qui-Gon had. He had that gift. What he needed to develop was Qui-Gon's wisdom. That would only take time and missions.

And mistakes. He could hear Qui-Gon's dry tone in his head.

The speeder was tweaked to run smoothly at high speeds, which Obi-Wan would expect from two Podracer owners. He sped back to the city core, Anakin at his side. He did not speculate on what was wrong. Whatever it was that had caused the panic in Bog's voice, he would know soon enough. He hoped nothing had happened to Astri or Didi.

They passed through the high-security gate on the outskirts of the Games Quarters, where athletes and officials were housed. Obi-Wan was relieved when he arrived to see Astri and Didi standing nearby as Bog talked earnestly to Siri and Ferus. Tru stood next to Ry-Gaul. Siri turned to greet him with a thinly disguised look of disgust on her face.

Obi-Wan leaped out of the speeder. "What happened?"

"Bog's speeder was stolen," Siri said. "He felt an alert to all Jedi teams was justified." Ry-Gaul sighed.

Obi-Wan gave Bog an exasperated glance. "You called in Jedi help because of a missing speeder?"

"You don't understand," Bog said. "The speeder was in a secure area. This is serious. I would think the Jedi would be concerned."

"There will always be petty crime at a large event

like this one," Siri said. "Everyone should be careful with their personal property."

"Petty?" Bog flushed. "I don't call this petty."

"What Siri means is that this is really a case for the planet security," Obi-Wan said.

Bog flourished his comlink. "Really? Let's see what Liviani says when she arrives."

"You called Liviani?" Obi-Wan asked.

"Of course. As the head of the Council of the Games, I thought she would want to know," Bog said. "I must remind you that I am a member."

"I don't think you need to remind them," Astri said in a low tone. "You keep mentioning it."

A gleaming black airspeeder drew up, and Liviani slid out. "I received your message," she told Bog in a concerned tone. "Tell me again what happened and what exactly is missing."

Bog threw the Jedi a triumphant look. "The speeder was gone when Astri and I returned from the opening rituals," he said. "As I told you, some personal possessions were inside. My green cloak — the only one I brought for warmth — and a box of my favorite figda candy, as well as my datapad, my travel kit . . . and I am sure other important things."

"This is very bad," Liviani said. "I'm glad you contacted me." Obi-Wan was surprised at the concern in her tone. He had expected her to be as annoyed as they were. "Members of the Council for the Games deserve the highest consideration." She turned to the Jedi. "You must investigate this at once."

Siri looked startled. "Investigate a speeder theft? It's a waste of our time."

Siri was never one to hide her feelings. "Surely there are better uses for our time," Obi-Wan said in a more conciliatory tone.

"I don't think so," Liviani said flatly. "Begin at once."

"We don't take orders from you," Siri said. Her face was calm but two bright red spots appeared on her cheeks. "We are here at the Ruling Power's request."

"Then I shall contact the Ruling Power," Liviani snapped, reaching for her comlink. "All I have to do is contact Maxo Vista. He will go to them at once, and they will order you."

"No one orders the Jedi." Ry-Gaul spoke at last. His soft voice was measured, but with a core of strength that made everyone stop and look at him. "We accept requests. Then we decide."

Liviani struggled to control her irritation. It was clear that Ry-Gaul's authoritative tone had made her realize it was time to back down. "Of course," she said through tight lips. She shoved her comlink back into her cloak pocket. "Then I *request* that this be investigated." She spoke in a more conciliatory tone. "Think about it. This area is under top security. Yet a thief entered and stole a valuable item. The athletes and workers are under my care."

Obi-Wan nodded shortly. "In that case, we accept your request. One Jedi team will investigate."

Liviani swept off in a swirl of robes and scarves. Siri drew closer to Obi-Wan.

"I still say this is a waste of time," she said. "Who knows how long it will take to investigate a theft?"

"I do," Obi-Wan said. "It will take exactly ten seconds." Then he looked hard at Didi, who coughed and looked away.

CHAPTER EIGHT

Anakin saw his Master signal to Didi. Didi tried to ignore the signal, but Obi-Wan strode over. Anakin followed curiously.

Obi-Wan drew Didi aside. "You'd better start talking fast," he said. "And no excuses. No diversions. Just the truth."

"I didn't steal it, I borrowed it," Didi said.

Didi had stolen his own son-in-law's speeder? Anakin couldn't believe it.

"I was going to return it," Didi said quickly, as he noted the thunderous expression on Obi-Wan's face.

"The same way you were going to return the credits?"

"Ah, you see!" Didi cried triumphantly. "My point exactly! How could I return the credits if I didn't steal the speeder?"

"Explain your logic," Obi-Wan said. "Nobody else can follow it."

"I was going to take your excellent advice and confess everything to Astri," Didi said. "I was on my way to find her and I saw the speeder. I began to reflect on the amount of credits I had borrowed, and the fact that if Bog found out he would no doubt banish me to wander the galaxy friendless and alone. So I thought it best to return the credits without his ever finding out."

"So you stole his speeder."

"*Borrowed.* But only so I could repay the credits! You see?"

"Well," Obi-Wan said, "you're just going to have to return it."

"Ah," Didi said. "Another excellent suggestion. Except it's too late. I've sold the speeder."

"At least then you can give them the credits," Obi-Wan said with a sigh.

"But I can't! I have to place another bet!"

Obi-Wan turned away. "Fine. I'm no longer involved. I'm telling Bog who stole the speeder, and you can explain it any way you want."

"Wait!" Didi screeched hurriedly. "My good friend,

Obi-Wan! You don't understand! I will return the speeder most definitely! My bet is a sure thing."

"No bet is a sure thing, Didi," Obi-Wan said. "When are you going to learn that?"

"But this one is! I promise!"

Obi-Wan paused. Anakin watched his face. He had expected his Master to walk away, but something Didi said had stopped him. It seemed a minor problem to Anakin. Why was Obi-Wan getting involved?

"How do you know the bet is a sure thing?" Obi-Wan asked.

Didi looked uncomfortable under Obi-Wan's scrutiny. "Well. You might say I have a tip."

"What kind of tip?" Obi-Wan frowned.

"A tip that an event is fixed," Didi admitted. "From a source I trust."

"Who?" Obi-Wan demanded.

"Someone you know," Didi said. "Fligh."

Obi-Wan groaned. "Not Fligh. Is he on Euceron?"

"Of course," Didi said. "Isn't everyone? And you can't beat Fligh's information. If there's a nasty, secret bit of business, you can bet Fligh knows about it. So how could I ignore his advice? The swoop obstacle race is fixed and I know the winner. If you'd let me make the bet, everything will be fine. My problems will be solved, and I know how much you want this."

"Wait here," Obi-Wan told him sternly.

He drew Anakin aside. "I think we should pursue this," he said. "If some of the events are fixed, it could cause major trouble. It could be a serious disruption of the peace."

We're wasting time on this. I could be with the Podracers. I could be helping Doby and Deland. They are trying to free their sister. Didi is trying to win a bet. Which is more important?

Anakin hid his disappointment with a frown. "Who is Fligh? Do you trust him?"

"Trust him?" Obi-Wan grimaced. "Not at all. But if he's heard something, we could have problems even if his information is false. Fligh hangs around the Senate. He knows everyone and passes along information for credits. If he's heard an event is fixed, he isn't the only one who thinks this." He sighed. "As much as I'd like to walk away from this, I'm afraid we'll have to investigate." Obi-Wan gave Anakin a careful look. "What is wrong, Padawan?"

"It seems . . . a waste of time to me," Anakin said, reluctant to contradict his Master. "We are here as peacekeepers. There is a better use of Jedi time." He did not mention Doby and Deland, but he knew his Master would know what he was not saying.

Obi-Wan nodded as if considering Anakin's opinion. "What do you think would be a better use of our time?"

Anakin looked down and said nothing.

"Tell me," Obi-Wan continued, "what do you think would happen if it was discovered that some of the events are fixed?"

Anakin shrugged. "Some will be upset. Especially those who have placed illegal bets."

"What about the planets involved? If it appears that some have cheated, or conspired to defraud the Games, how will other worlds react? Each world sends the very best of its athletes to compete in the Games. These beings are often great heroes on their homeworlds. What if they are denied their victories because an event is fixed?"

"I guess it could create some unrest," Anakin said, after a pause.

"Yes, young Padawan," Obi-Wan said. "Hundreds of thousands of beings are crammed into one city. All have come to cheer their heroes or their future heroes. It may not seem an important lead for us to follow, but missions don't always start out with a battle. Sometimes they begin with something insignificant. Something unimportant. Part of being a Jedi is to recognize the small thing that can change everything."

"If it is so small, how can we recognize it?"

"We take ourselves out of what we are looking at," Obi-Wan answered.

Anakin scowled. "I don't understand."

Obi-Wan put his hand on Anakin's shoulder. "I know. That is why you are still a Padawan. Someday you will."

CHAPTER NINE

Obi-Wan didn't blame Anakin for his puzzlement. Didi's bet didn't appear to be worth Jedi investigation. But instinct was ticking inside Obi-Wan, telling him that this was something to pursue. He had learned not to ignore that small voice. Qui-Gon had taught him that. If he could teach Anakin one thing, it would be to slow down enough to hear that insistent sound, sometimes no more than a whisper, that said, *follow this.*

Didi nervously scuttled through the crowded streets, his eyes alert for the security force he was sure would be pursuing him soon. "It occurs to me that Fligh might not be too pleased to hear that I have involved the Jedi," he said. "Perhaps it would be better if you went on alone."

"No, it wouldn't," Obi-Wan answered firmly.

Didi stopped and turned. "Do not take this wrong. I am honored and blessed with your presence. But being friends with you is not easy, Obi-Wan."

"I know."

Didi turned into a crowded open-air plaza. Fountains played in the center, each one displaying the colors of a different world and changing in the next instant to another, so that the sparkling water seemed to glow with a thousand colors at once. Trees and bushes from planets around the galaxy had been placed in huge stone urns that offered shade for the chairs and tables set up underneath. A large screen flashed the opening times of various events, as well as the best routes to get to them. Other smaller screens showed events taking place in the various stadiums. Beings from around the galaxy sat watching the screens, sipping juice or tea, eating sweets, and watching children play in the multicolored fountains. A four-piece band played soft jizz-wail music.

Obi-Wan's glance swept the plaza. Although he had not seen Fligh in many years, he recognized him immediately. He sat with his back to a wall snaked with blooming vines, tapping one long foot to the music. He sipped from a glass of bright yellow juice. He was as thin and spidery as ever, and his long ears appeared even longer, the lobes resting on his shoulders. A tuft of graying yellow hair sprouted from his balding head. Several gold rings were stacked on his long fingers. As they came closer, Obi-Wan saw that Fligh had replaced his pride and joy — his fake green eye — with a bright gold one.

Obi-Wan had first met Fligh when he was Qui-Gon's Padawan. Fligh had sworn to help his best friend Didi even as he squirmed out of telling the truth to the Jedi and faked his own death. Getting the whole truth out of Fligh wouldn't be easy.

His pleasant expression darkened with apprehension when he saw the Jedi, but he quickly turned it into a welcoming smile. "Didi! Old friend! Such a surprise to see you on Euceron! Though everyone who is anyone is here, so there you go, not such a surprise after all."

"Do you remember Obi-Wan Kenobi, the great Jedi Knight?"

"Ah, but he was just a Learner when I knew him," Fligh said. "Obi-Wan, what a fortunate meeting! It is my luck to be able to renew our great friendship."

"We were never friends," Obi-Wan pointed out.

"We weren't, it's true, and that is a pity," Fligh agreed sadly. "But now we have a second chance. I see that now you have a Padawan Learner yourself."

"I am Anakin Skywalker," Anakin said.

Fligh turned to examine him curiously with his good eye. "I have heard about you."

Anakin looked defensive. "What have you heard?"

"Whoa-hoa, relax, young friend," Fligh said. "It was all good things, I assure you. Yes, promising Jedi, amazing talents, there you go."

"Didi tells us you have some information about some of the events at the Games," Obi-Wan said.

Fligh narrowed his eye at Didi. "Do I? I hear things, but nothing important enough to involve the Jedi."

"That is not what Didi said." Obi-Wan stood casually, as though he had all the time in the world, but he was prepared to pressure Fligh. He was impatient to get to the bottom of this. He didn't want to waste more of the day.

"All right, all right," Didi said when Fligh shot him another look. "I told him. But he's a Jedi, Fligh. You can't lie to a Jedi."

"I don't see why not," Fligh shot back, too angry to watch his words. "They're no different from anybody else."

"Oh, yes," Anakin said stridently. "We are."

Fligh's head whipped around, his ears taking a moment to catch up. They bobbed gently and came to rest on his shoulders. His gaze flicked to the lightsabers tucked into Obi-Wan's and Anakin's belts. "Errrrr, you do

have a point. There you go. I concede it. In that case —
and considering our deep friendship which I cherish despite your refusal to acknowledge it — I will tell you
what I know. I heard a rumor that one of the events was
fixed. I told Didi about it. After all, why shouldn't my
friend benefit?" He gave Didi a hard stare. "If I'd known
that friend had such a big mouth, I might have recon-
sidered."

"Are you involved in this?" Obi-Wan asked him. "Do
you know who fixed the obstacle race, and how?"

"I know nothing except this — the participant from
Alderaan will win."

Obi-Wan frowned. How could a swoop obstacle
race — a series of timed individual races against the
clock — be fixed? "How do you know?"

"I don't have to tell you that," Fligh said defiantly.

"That's true," Obi-Wan said. "But you will have to tell
the security force for the Ruling Power."

Fligh broke into a smile. "No need for that! I'd much
rather share with friends! I was told by Quentor. A being
very much like me, who does similar work."

"Another thief?"

"Another businessman like myself, who buys and
sells information and the occasional valuable item that
might find its way into our hands. Quentor would not tell
me how he knew, but he swore the information was

true, and I believed him. A clever one, that Quentor. He would not steer you wrong. He swore that there is an insider at the Games who has arranged to fix an event. A good way to make a quick fortune, isn't it? I thought it was a rumor worth a few gambling credits for myself and my friend."

Obi-Wan considered this. Fligh was calling it a rumor, but he had told Didi to bet and no doubt had placed a bet himself. But that didn't necessarily mean the rumor was true. Didi had placed plenty of bad bets, some of them on Fligh's advice.

Fligh saw Obi-Wan's hesitation. "You might want to place a bet yourself, my friend. Even the Jedi can use wealth. You could stop hitching rides and have your own transports, maybe invest in some new robes —"

Obi-Wan turned and searched the event board. "The event is starting soon."

"Yes, unfortunately too late for you to do anything about it," Fligh said. "So sorry. There you go."

"Stadium Five. It's not far," Obi-Wan said. "Come on, Anakin. You too, Didi."

"Not me, surely," Didi said. "I need to visit with my old friend — oooooohhh!" Obi-Wan had grabbed his collar and yanked him into step next to the Jedi.

"We can make it," Obi-Wan said. "We have four minutes."

They hurried from the plaza. The streets had emptied as various events had begun. Obi-Wan and Anakin quickened their pace, so Didi had a hard time keeping up. Obi-Wan was reluctant to let him go. There was no way to keep track of Fligh, but they could at least keep hold of Didi, their tie to Fligh.

"There's an air taxi!" Didi called, breathing hard. "I beg you, Obi-Wan, take it!"

Obi-Wan signaled and the air taxi zoomed to a stop. It was empty except for the pilot.

"The swoop obstacle course event, Stadium Five," Obi-Wan said.

The pilot nodded without turning and glided back into the air lane. Obi-Wan settled back into a seat next to Anakin.

"What will we do when we get there?" Anakin asked him in a low tone.

"I'm not sure yet," Obi-Wan said. "We can't say for sure the event is fixed. We can't make that accusation without more proof."

The ship's velocity pushed him back against the seat. Buildings were a blur of bright color as they flashed by.

"Isn't he going a trifle fast?" Didi asked, pressing his hands together.

"Master, I feel a disturbance in the Force," Anakin murmured.

Obi-Wan had been startled by the same feeling. He rose and started toward the pilot, but the cruiser jerked violently to the left, almost throwing him to the floor. He grabbed a pole and righted himself, then started toward the pilot again. The ship veered to the right, grazing a sign. Metal shrieked and the cruiser lurched again. Didi fell off his seat with a yelp.

Obi-Wan fought his way to the front of the taxi as the ship careened down the road, clipping branches, signs, and narrowly missing buildings. Then the pilot reversed the engines and zoomed down another spacelane . . . the wrong way.

Cruisers were heading straight for them. The pilot pushed the speed to maximum and jumped to his feet. He balanced for a moment on the lip of the air taxi, then calmly leaped into the air. He was wearing an anti-grav propulsion belt, so he dropped quickly but safely to the ground, leaving them in a runaway cruiser screaming the wrong way down an air lane.

"We're going to die!" Didi screamed.

CHAPTER TEN

Anakin vaulted over the rows of seats and landed in the pilot's chair, his hands already outstretched for the controls. In midair, he had seen precisely what he needed to do.

A less-experienced pilot would have immediately reduced speed. Anakin knew better. He needed the speed to avoid the collision. Instead of slowing, he made a hard right. The cruiser passed them by, so close Anakin could see the fearful gaze of the pilot, who did not have the time or reflexes to alter his course.

The air taxi was slower and clumsier than a Podracer, but Anakin felt the familiar thrill of pushing a machine to its limits as he negotiated tight spaces at high speeds.

As soon as they were past the cruiser, Anakin reduced speed while turning to the left. He had just enough speed to avoid the next collision. Then he kept the air taxi turning until they were facing in the correct direction. Anakin calmly joined the stream of traffic.

Didi spoke from the floor, his head in his hands. "Are we dead yet?"

"Good piloting, Padawan." Obi-Wan sank into a seat behind Anakin. "That was close."

Didi rose shakily to his feet. "What kind of a pilot tries to crash an air taxi and then jumps off? I've had some bad air-taxi drivers, but . . ." He looked at the Jedi. "No. No, no."

"Yes," Obi-Wan said. "It was deliberate. We were definitely targeted. Most likely by Fligh."

Didi shook his head. "Not Fligh. He's my friend."

"Well, your *friend* told someone we were on our way to the stadium," Anakin said. "That empty air taxi didn't show up by accident."

Warning lights suddenly flashed behind them and a voice boomed. "Pull over. Ruling Power security. Repeat. Pull over."

"You'd better do it," Obi-Wan told Anakin. "We're going to have to explain this."

"Security!" Didi exclaimed. "You don't need me, do you, Obi-Wan? I can go to the stadium and report to you what goes on —"

"If I hear you placed a bet, you will regret it," Obi-Wan warned him.

"No bets!" Didi stood by the door, waiting for Anakin to slow enough for him to jump off. "Promise!"

Anakin slowed the craft, and Didi leaped off and disappeared into the crowd as the security officers exited their Flash Speeder and approached the Jedi.

The security officer was dressed completely in black. He flipped up the visor of his shiny helmet.

"We received reports of a runaway air taxi endangering traffic."

"We are Jedi," Obi-Wan said. "The pilot exited and disappeared, and we got the taxi under control."

The officer studied them for a moment, then entered the information into his palm-sized datapad. "Description?"

Obi-Wan gave his estimates of height and weight. "He was dressed in the regulation air-taxi pilot uniform," he said. "He had a reflective visor on his helmet, so his features were obscured, but he appeared to be a humanoid. Left earlobe slightly larger than the right. A tear on the third knuckle of his right glove. He was right-handed."

"One boot had a two-centimeter slash in the leather near the instep," Anakin supplied. "Dark matter on the right glove."

"Possibly blood, but there was no evidence of injury, so we could assume it was from another being," Obi-Wan interjected. "Sour smell indicates he had recently exerted himself. Perhaps from the battle to commandeer the air taxi. You'll probably find an injured air-taxi pilot."

"We already have. He gave a description. He said the guy was tall." The officer tucked the datapad into his belt. "Never believed that stuff about Jedi. Now I do. Larger left earlobe, huh?" He shook his head. "It's good information, but the city is packed. We might not find him. You can proceed."

Stadium Five was now only steps away. Obi-Wan and Anakin hurried through the tall arches and into the open-air arena. Their ears rang with the noise of a roaring crowd. The race had already begun.

Didi had entered the same way and was waiting for them by the refreshment stand while watching the race on a monitor. Obi-Wan saw that the large circular track was made up of many levels, from the floor of the arena to the top. Each level had a series of holographic obstacles for the swoops to avoid or evade, such as trees, creatures, and traffic officers. He hurried over. "Did they ask about Bog's speeder?"

"No, they were only interested in the air taxi," Obi-Wan said. "Has anything odd happened?"

"Nothing that I can see. All the swoops are performing well. The Alderaan pilot is in the lead." Didi wrung his hands. "And to think I could have bet on him!"

Obi-Wan strode toward a viewing platform. The noise of the crowd reverberated off the walls of the stadium and caused the air to ring against his ears. He was high above the race below. The agile swoops, wearing different planetary colors, zoomed around holographic obstacles that suddenly appeared in their paths. The crowd roared approval or fury at the spectacle.

Obi-Wan watched carefully. The swoops seemed to be functioning perfectly. The pilots were battling with every ounce of concentration they possessed.

"It has to be the timers," he murmured to Anakin. "Someone must have tampered with them. Only a hundredth of a second off, and the race will be won."

"Are the timers controlled by one person?" Anakin asked.

"I don't know," Obi-Wan said. "But we can find out."

The race ended with the Alderaan pilot zooming past the finish line to cheers and boos. Beside Obi-Wan, Didi groaned.

"There goes my fortune," he said.

A viewing platform glided into the center of the stadium. A tall, handsome Euceron male held a flashing hologram embedded in crystal over his head. It was the first-place award. The crowd went wild.

"It's Maxo Vista," Didi breathed in tones of awe.

Anakin peered across the distance. "He's older than I thought."

"He is magnificent," Didi said.

"Didi, I want you to do something for me," Obi-Wan said, turning his back on the award ceremony. "First of all, stay out of trouble. Second, stick close to Fligh. I might need to talk to him again."

"All right, Obi-Wan. I will do what you say. My fate is intertwined with your desires," Didi said, his sad eyes still on the ceremony.

"Let us go, Padawan," Obi-Wan said. "I'd like to have a word with the timekeeper for this event."

On the way to the exclusive VIP skybox on Level Twenty where the Games Council members and other officials sat, Obi-Wan contacted the keeper of the Archives, Jocasta Nu, at the Temple.

"Can you do a quick search for me on a being named Quentor? Your basic operator who hangs around the Senate. He trades in information and stolen goods."

"What do you need to know?" Jocasta Nu asked.

"I'm not sure. His whereabouts, for one thing. Any

ties he might have to the Ruling Power of Euceron or the Galactic Games."

As he spoke, Obi-Wan stepped inside the Council skybox. In the first row of the box, Maxo Vista was talking to a tall Euceron dressed in a long white robe. Obi-Wan assumed the Euceron was a Ruler, but he didn't know which one. He hung back for a moment.

"Can we meet him? Can we meet Maxo Vista?" Anakin whispered, close by his side. He had heard stories of how Vista performed in the last Games.

"Maxo Vista?" Jocasta Nu asked, overhearing Anakin. Her voice lost its businesslike quality. Obi-Wan had never heard her sound so warm. "Have you met him?"

"No," Obi-Wan said.

"You don't know who he is, do you?" Jocasta Nu demanded.

"Can you retrieve that information for me?" Obi-Wan asked irritably.

"Yes, Obi-Wan. I'll do what I can." Jocasta Nu's voice brimmed with humor, an unusual occurrence.

Maxo Vista caught sight of them and came forward with the tall Euceron. "I have hoped to meet the Jedi," he said. "This is Ruler Three, one of the esteemed Ruling Power."

Obi-Wan introduced himself and Anakin. Maxo Vista

flashed a charismatic smile, his vivid green eyes shining. "We are grateful that the Jedi have graciously agreed to attend the Games. With so many worlds coming together for these Games, it holds out a promise for peace throughout the galaxy."

Ruler Three bowed. "Our government thanks you. Now I must attend the next event."

As soon as Ruler Three had left, Obi-Wan turned back to Maxo Vista. "We would like to speak with the official timekeeper for this event."

"Of course." Maxo leaned forward to touch a glowing screen. "That would be Aarno Dering." He peered over at a glass skybox with an excellent view of the action. "He's already left, I'm afraid. But I can give you his room number at the official Games quarters."

"We'd appreciate it."

Maxo Vista hesitated. "Is anything wrong?"

"Just a routine check," Obi-Wan assured him.

He nodded and consulted the screen again, then gave them Aarno Dering's location. Obi-Wan and Anakin hurried out of Stadium Five. The air taxis were full of the departing crowd. Obi-Wan and Anakin threaded through the crowd, moving quickly and easily through the crush.

"I can't believe I actually met Maxo Vista," Anakin said. "I'll never forget his performance in the swoop races in the last Games. And did you see him in the holographic obstacle course? He set a new galactic record." Obi-Wan's face was blank, and Anakin sighed. "I can't believe you don't know who he is. Everybody —"

"— knows Maxo Vista," Obi-Wan finished. "But right now I'm more interested in Aarno Dering."

At the quarters, they passed the security checkpoint and quickly accessed a map for directions to Block Seven, Room 4116.

"This way," Obi-Wan said.

They hurried down the outdoor walkways that connected the various temporary buildings built of hard duraplastoid materials in bright colors. When they reached Block Seven, they took a moving walkway up to the fourth story.

"Room 4116 should be at the end of the walkway," Anakin said.

A tall humanoid male came out of a door at the end of the walkway. He paused while he carefully placed various personal items in different-sized pockets. His neutral gaze slid over the surrounding area and lit on the Jedi.

He jumped and a look of surprised panic lit his eyes. He turned abruptly and headed the other way.

"Aarno Dering?" Obi-Wan called, quickening his pace. "We'd like to talk to you."

Dering began to run. Obi-Wan and Anakin leaped forward in a surge of speed.

Dering had a good head start, but he was no athlete. He leaped onto the moving walkway and zigzagged past athletes and workers, pushing some aside roughly. Obi-Wan leaped off the second story and landed lightly on the ground. Anakin followed.

When Dering raced out an exit from the quarters and into the street, Obi-Wan was merely steps away. Suddenly, a fast-moving airspeeder headed straight for Dering. Obi-Wan reached out, ready to grab the waving hem of the man's tunic, but the speeder struck the slight man first, sending him flying through the air. Aarno Dering landed with a sickening thud.

CHAPTER ELEVEN

"Go to him," Obi-Wan ordered Anakin tersely.

Obi-Wan jumped after the speeder. Landing on the speeder's outrigger component, Obi-Wan drew his lightsaber and severed it with one stroke. The speeder veered and crashed into a bright yellow bench, and the pilot leaped out. Obi-Wan recognized him instantly as the pilot of the air taxi. Something about the way he held his body alerted him. His movements were quick and powerful, but loose and graceful as well.

The pilot leaped over the speeder and raced down the street. Without breaking stride, he shot a cable launcher up to the roof of a high building. The cable launcher pulled him up and he disappeared onto the roof.

Obi-Wan activated his own launcher and followed,

the wind rushing past his ears. He jumped onto the roof just as the pilot leaped to the next building. Obi-Wan followed.

The pilot never looked back. Obi-Wan noted his coolness. There were not many, being pursued, who did not pause to check on the location of their pursuer. Obi-Wan was gaining and the pilot seemed to know it, for his pace quickened as he leaped to the next roof. It was twenty meters below, but he landed easily and kept on running. Obi-Wan summoned the Force for his jump and landed.

The pilot raced to the edge of the roof that overlooked the street. Obi-Wan could hear the noise of a crowd and as he drew closer he saw that a stadium below was emptying. Air taxis were lined up awaiting passengers. The pilot paused and activated his anti-grav propulsion belt. It allowed him to drop off the roof and land safely on the walkway below.

Obi-Wan leaped down and had to swerve at the last moment to avoid a child who suddenly darted out from between her mother and father. He landed hard. He was just in time to see the pilot get swallowed up by the surging crowd.

Irritation flamed and died away. He would have liked to have caught the pilot. It did not happen. On to the next.

He made his way back to the quarters. Anakin knelt by Aarno Dering, his hand on the man's shoulder. Obi-Wan knew immediately that he was dead.

He walked to Anakin and put his hand on the boy's shoulder. They stood for a moment, a linked chain of commemoration. A Jedi always paused to reflect on a life lost, even if they did not know the spirit who had left.

"There was nothing I could do." Anakin's face was pale. He had seen death before, but he was still affected by it. Obi-Wan was glad to see this. He hoped Anakin would never lose that particular vulnerability. There had been a time when he had wondered if Anakin failed to connect, a time when he had seen a curious blankness on the boy's face after he had killed in battle. Since that time, Obi-Wan had watched Anakin carefully. When he saw his Padawan feel the enormity of a life lost, he was reassured.

A security speeder pulled up, its signal lights flashing. Close behind was the sleek black airspeeder of Liviani Sarno. When she jumped out, it was clear she was livid.

"First an air-taxi driver is badly beaten, and now this," she snapped, standing over the body of Aarno Dering. "How will you explain this to the Council?"

Anakin flushed with anger, and Obi-Wan's hand tightened on his shoulder. Liviani Sarno's words had offended Obi-Wan as well. She treated the death of a fellow being as a nasty inconvenience.

"Obviously the Jedi cannot fulfill their promises," Liviani continued.

"The Jedi promised nothing except our presence," Obi-Wan said.

Her lips pressed together. "In that case, I am calling for extra security."

"That is a good idea," Obi-Wan answered. He was nettled at her tone, but extra security was not a bad idea. He didn't want to reveal his suspicions to Liviani yet. Officials had a tendency to get in the way. Obi-Wan wanted to make sure of what he was dealing with first.

Liviani turned to confer with a security officer. "I suggest you find an event to attend," she said over her shoulder to the Jedi. "Just stand around and do nothing. If you can manage that much."

Obi-Wan strode away. Anakin let out a long breath.

"I have more things to learn about patience," he said. "I don't know how you keep your temper sometimes, Master."

"Indulging momentary irritation is nothing more than a distraction," Obi-Wan answered. "Liviani is worried that if disruptions occur it will reflect badly on her. We have more important things to do. When Aarno Dering left his room, did you notice anything significant?"

He watched as his Padawan frowned, thinking. Then Anakin's face brightened.

"He was just sliding his datapad into his tunic with his left hand. He dropped it when he saw us. It fell in the doorway and the door did not shut."

"Exactly," Obi-Wan said. "I think we might want to take a peek into the life of Aarno Dering."

They passed through the security gate again and quickly made their way to Dering's room. It was only a matter of time before the security officers arrived. Obi-Wan wasn't sure how cooperative they would be with the Jedi.

The datapad lay in the doorway. Obi-Wan handed it to Anakin and reached down for a small folder that had been dropped as well. In it was a text doc ID for someone named Ak Duranc.

"It's a false text doc for Aarno Dering," he told Anakin. "Often new identities use the same initials as the being's real name. It helps them to remember their new identity."

"But what does it mean?" Anakin asked. "Why would Dering want a new identity?"

"There's only one reason," Obi-Wan said. "He was

afraid he would get caught. The question is why." He tapped the text doc thoughtfully against his leg. "Beings don't go to this much trouble without cause. He was afraid. But of what?"

Obi-Wan surveyed the room. It was small and neat. Everything was put away. A closed travel pack sat on a table. Two chronos sat by the sleep couch. Obi-Wan picked them up.

"They are set to wake him up," he said. "He used two so that he would not oversleep." He placed them back where he'd found them. "Interesting. A chrono expert who does not trust chronos."

"Master, look at this." Anakin bent over a holofile. "He didn't code any of his files."

"He was worried enough to get a new identity, but he didn't have time to code his files," Obi-Wan mused. "That meant he was once confident that he wouldn't get caught."

"He's noted the events that he's set up the timing system for. The bowcaster skill contest and holographic obstacle course are the only ones left. But Master . . ." Anakin looked up. "The Podrace is here, too."

Obi-Wan came over and studied the file. "So. Whoever is behind fixing the games could be fixing the Podrace, too."

Anakin tapped the datapad. "This means that Doby

and Deland don't stand a chance. The winner has already been chosen."

"Possibly. We don't know anything for sure yet."

"What I don't understand is how a Podrace can be fixed," Anakin continued. "It's not like an obstacle swoop race, where individual segments are timed. Whoever crosses the finish line first wins. You can't guarantee that someone won't crack up or crash. I wouldn't take the bet, even if someone told me the race was fixed."

Obi-Wan nodded. "I see what you mean. But it can't be a coincidence that the corrupt timing judge has agreed to time the race." He stared at the neat belongings of Aarno Dering while he considered their next step. He knew it was inevitable, but he didn't like it. He would have to send Anakin back to the Podracers.

"This could be a larger-scale operation than I thought," he said aloud. "No doubt Fligh didn't tell us everything. And no doubt there are parts to this that even Fligh doesn't know. I will contact Siri and Ry-Gaul to see if they have discovered anything. Anakin, you must go back to the Podracers." Obi-Wan did not like the way Anakin's face brightened at this. "You have made friends with Doby and Deland. See if they know how the race could be fixed and if there is heavy betting going on."

"And what will you do, Master?"

"I'm going to work from the opposite end. If we want to find out who is fixing the events, we have to find out who benefits. That means that someone, or a group of beings, are placing bets on the outcome."

"But how can you discover who that is?"

"I have to reacquaint myself with Uso Yso."

CHAPTER TWELVE

Anakin piloted Doby and Deland's speeder back to the Podrace hangar, leaving Obi-Wan as he checked in with Siri and Ry-Gaul to see if other complications had sprung up. Anakin was glad that the investigation had allowed him to return. He already felt that Doby and Deland were friends. He'd made a promise to them, and he intended to keep it. The best part was that he could do this and still follow Obi-Wan's instructions. Working on their Podracer would be the perfect cover for him to keep his eyes and ears open.

But if he were honest with himself, Anakin had to admit that it wasn't just his promise and the mission that drove him back to the Podracer. It was how good it felt to be here. Here he did not have to worry if he was good enough. He did not need to question himself.

All he had to do was make something go very, very fast.

He saw Doby and Deland working on the engine as he parked the speeder and hurried over. Deland raised a grease-stained face. "Am I glad to see you! We have a rotor problem we can't seem to fix."

"Let me have a look." Anakin leaned over the engine. "This could be a connector problem. Let me take a look at the valves. Hand me that hydrospanner, will you?"

Anakin took the hydrospanner from Doby and bent over the engine. "Have you run the track in a speeder yet?" he asked. "An advance look is always a good idea." The more information he got about the race, the easier it would be to figure out how it was fixed.

"Can't," Doby said. "The Podracers won't know the track until they're racing."

Anakin looked up. "What do you mean?"

"The onboard nav computer will flash us the next area of the track every three minutes," Deland explained. "We have to race and navigate at the same time. It's a new innovation that Sebulba dreamed up."

"He knows Hekula can do it, with his reflexes," Doby said. "Plus they have such a maneuverable Podracer. The rest of us have had to reconfigure a bit, but it sure does make the race more exciting."

Anakin tinkered with the valves. Could this be the

key to how the race was fixed? What if Sebulba's Podracer got the track information before anyone else? That would definitely give Hekula an edge.

"Who sends the route to the onboard computers?" he asked.

"The official timekeeper set up the program," Doby said. "Don't know his name."

But I do. It's Aarno Dering. And Aarno Dering is dead. Someone else will have to run the program. But who?

"Who's the favorite?" Anakin asked. "How are the odds running?"

"Ten to one for Hekula," Deland said. "Rumor has it that Sebulba has bet a fortune on his son."

Of course he has. He knows Hekula will win.

Anakin glanced over the hood of the Podracer to where Sebulba was sitting, sipping tea while the pit droids worked on Hekula's Podracer. Sebulba looked over and met his eyes. Something happened behind the creature's bulging eyes. Memory clicked in.

He rose, his front arms waving, and approached. "Now I recognize you, slave boy. All you needed was a little grease on your face." He laughed. "What an unfortunate surprise. I thought you were dead."

"Not yet, Sebulba," Anakin shot back. "I'm here to make sure your son loses the way you did back on Tatooine. Badly."

"Luck was on your side that day, slave boy," Sebulba hissed. "You are just a human, slow and clumsy as a bantha. I should have killed you then."

"You tried," Anakin said coolly. "But you failed. Failure seems to be your destiny."

"Insolent boy!" Sebulba hissed, raising his hand for a blow. Anakin had no doubt that his blow would still be powerful enough to send him flying.

But he was a Jedi now. Sebulba's arm moved so fast it was a blur, but to Anakin it looked like slow-motion. He easily stepped aside in time. The wind fanned against his face. Sebulba staggered, his balance upset. He had expected to land the punch.

"You can't touch me," Anakin said. He whispered the words, close enough now to smell Sebulba's rank scent. "You were never fast enough. You still aren't."

"Slave boy!" Sebulba went toward him again. This time Anakin whirled and delivered a kick that sent Sebulba flying.

Enraged, Sebulba started toward a waiting Anakin, but suddenly the Glymphid Aldar Beedo stepped between them.

"You're disturbing my concentration," he said to Anakin, tapping a blaster on his belt.

"He's a Jedi," Doby whispered. "I wouldn't do that if I were you."

"All beings are the same once they're dead," Beedo said, his eyes cool.

Anakin hesitated, not sure what to do. The situation now threatened to spiral out of control. Hekula was starting across to join in. If a fight began, others could be hurt, including Doby and Deland.

"Master!" Suddenly Djulla appeared and tugged at Sebulba's robe. "I have made fresh tea."

"So what?" Sebulba said furiously. "Get away from me, slave!"

He struggled to kick Djulla aside with his hind legs while keeping his eyes on Anakin. Deland jumped forward to protect his sister. Sebulba's kick connected and Deland flew through the air, smashing against the cliff face. He landed awkwardly on his arm with a cry.

"Deland!" Djulla ran toward her brother. She knelt beside him. "You're hurt!"

"Get away from him!" Hekula suddenly roared, rushing forward. "You take orders from us! Get back to your post!"

Djulla hesitated. Aldar Beedo shrugged and turned away, tucking his blaster back into his belt. "This is a family matter," he said. "I have work to do."

Deland's teeth gritted. "Go back," he told his sister. "I am all right."

Hekula turned to Anakin. "If you keep insisting on making trouble, you'll be sorry."

Anakin trembled with the effort of holding himself back. He thought of Obi-Wan's coolness. He could not feel it, but he could imitate it. It was better to let this particular moment pass. He was not a slave boy, he was a Jedi. He could not pick a fight because two bullies deserved to be humiliated.

Djulla hurried away. Doby helped his brother to his feet. Deland held his arm carefully.

"Better get the medic, boy!" Sebulba called before scuttling back to his Podracer. "It looks like you won't be able to pilot your Podracer."

"He's right," Deland said through gritted teeth. "It's broken."

"What are we going to do?" Doby whispered. "This was our last chance. What can we do for Djulla now?"

Anakin saw the desperation on the two brothers' faces. Once again, he was faced with a choice. He had to make it for himself. He had to do the right thing and trust that Obi-Wan would understand.

"I can pilot the Podracer," he said. "If I win, your sister will go free."

"But that isn't fair," Doby said. "Why would you do such a thing?"

"Because it is the right thing to do," Anakin said.

He knew that from the bottom of his heart. But he still had to tell his Master.

CHAPTER THIRTEEN

Obi-Wan stood across the street from Uso Yso's swoop shop. He had disguised himself as a space traveler, pulling on a dull gray cloak and a wrapped headdress. As he watched, a steady stream of visitors entered and left the shop. None of them left with a swoop. Apparently Yso was doing a thriving business in taking illegal bets.

Obi-Wan saw a short, plump figure suddenly dart across the street and head for Yso's dark front door. He sprinted across the street to catch up.

He yanked Didi back by the collar of his tunic. "What are you doing?"

"Nothing. At least, nothing now, since you are holding my collar," Didi said.

"You said you were going to buy back Bog's speeder," Obi-Wan accused.

"I tried! I did! But the cheating monkey-lizard I sold it to upped the price," Didi told him. "I couldn't afford to buy back my own speeder! I need to raise a little cash, so I thought I would sell Bog's datapad and buy back his speeder instead."

Obi-Wan saw the datapad tucked under Didi's arm. "Let me see that."

There was a chance that someone on the Games Council knew the events were rigged. This might be an easy way to find out. He quickly accessed the information on Bog's system and flipped through random files. There didn't seem to be anything amiss. One file was labeled WAYS TO ADVANCE. Obi-Wan accessed it and read through a list of instructions Bog had written to himself.

BE FRIENDLY TO ALL!! THOSE WHO CANNOT HELP YOU TODAY CAN HELP YOU TOMORROW!!

DO MENIAL TASKS FOR IMPORTANT BEINGS!! IT MAKES YOU IN-DISPENSABLE!!

NEVER CONTRADICT A SUPERIOR!!

FOLLOW THE POWER!!!!!!!

"You see what I have to put up with?" Didi sighed. "My poor Astri."

Obi-Wan accessed another file marked GAMES COUNCIL

RESPONSIBILITIES. He scanned the notes carefully. It appeared that Bog's only job on the Games Council was arranging VIP seating. He had made lists matching Senators with exclusive gallery skyboxes for various events. So much for his importance.

Obi-Wan shut down the datapad. He tucked it inside his tunic.

"I was going to sell that!" Didi protested.

"It's not yours to sell. Didi, I know you won't take my advice. But things just might be more complicated than you realize. I'd advise you to stay away from betting."

"I assure you I will," Didi said, his brown eyes sincere.

Obi-Wan's comlink signaled. Jocasta Nu's voice came through crisply. He spoke so that Didi could not hear. "I found out who Quentor is. Were you playing a joke on me, Obi-Wan?" Jocasta Nu asked.

"No, of course not."

"There was no record of him anywhere, so I did the usual criminal search. Then a deep background trace. Nothing appeared."

"So he is an underground figure."

Jocasta Nu chuckled. "Not exactly. He's a yellow-tailed summerbird."

"He's a bird?"

"An unofficial pet of the Senate. He lives in the eaves of the building and the Senators leave him fruit and crumbs to feed on. If he's one of your suspects, I must warn you, he hasn't left Coruscant. He's most likely nibbling on muja fruit right about now."

Obi-Wan groaned, then thanked Jocasta Nu and cut the communication. Fligh had lied to him. That wasn't surprising. It was a lie worthy of Fligh, one calculated to delay him and amuse him.

But he wasn't amused.

He turned to Didi. "Do you know where Fligh is staying?"

Didi shook his head. "A guest house, I suppose. A hovel, I'm sure. Fligh is very cheap."

"Find out."

"Ah. Yes, Obi-Wan. I can see in your eyes that you need this information and I will not fail you." Didi bowed and rushed away.

Obi-Wan knocked on the door to Yso's shop, duplicating Didi's rhythmic knock. Someone hurried out, his face turned away. No one wanted to be recognized in this kind of place. Obi-Wan pretended to examine a beat-up swoop with a dented handlebar while he listened to the other occupant of the shop approach Uso Yso.

"I'd like to buy a swoop."

"At what price?"

The bettor named a figure, then said, "I'll take it to the blaster skill event where I hope to see Wesau T'orrin of Rezi-9 win."

"That is a good plan." Uso Yso slipped the credits into a wide belt he wore around his waist and entered some information into a datapad. He handed the bettor a small durasheet. "Here is your receipt."

Obi-Wan waited until the bettor had left the shop, then approached. "I'm here for a swoop," he said, looking up at the tall being. He waved a hand. "I would like to see your datapad."

Uso Yso snorted. "You don't need to see my datapad to buy a swoop. Which do you want?"

Obi-Wan waved his hand again. Uso Yso was unusually resistant to Jedi mind suggestion. "I'd like to see your datapad first."

"If you don't want to buy a swoop, you can leave," Uso Yso said, his eyes narrowing in suspicion.

Obi-Wan suppressed his slight disappointment. No matter how adept a Jedi was or how strong the connection to the Force, sometimes mind suggestion just didn't work.

Obi-Wan followed the lead of the bettor, naming a figure, then saying, "I plan to take the swoop to the Podrace and hope that Deland Tyerell will be the winner."

Uso Yso shook his head. "There's been a last-minute change. A new driver. Do you still want the swoop?"

"Who is the driver?" Obi-Wan asked curiously.

Yso consulted his datapad. "Anakin Skywalker."

Obi-Wan felt the shock shimmer inside him, but he did not register surprise on his face.

"Well?" Yso demanded impatiently.

Before Obi-Wan could answer, a small, slight being with four eyes, two of them set on the sides of his head, slipped inside the shop. "Security patrol outside."

Uso Yso pushed a lever and a wall slid back, revealing more swoops in various stages of repair. "Besum!" He tossed a tool kit to his assistant. "Start working."

"I don't know how to fix a swoop!"

"I don't care," Yso snarled. "Just do it." He turned to Obi-Wan. "Security makes patrols every once in a while. Nothing to worry about."

Now that Yso was in danger of losing Obi-Wan's business, he was suddenly friendly. He had also left his datapad angled toward Obi-Wan, and the notations were easy to read. In the time it took for Yso to check on Besum's activities, Obi-Wan had scanned the file and memorized it.

To his surprise, the letters and numbers looked familiar. It took him only a moment to realize that they were similar to the notes recording the skybox seating on Bog's datapad.

Which meant that Bog wasn't recording seats for Senators. He was recording bets.

CHAPTER FOURTEEN

Obi-Wan left the shop and found a quiet alley to pe-
ruse Bog's files. He read the names of the Senators
who had the same notations as Yso's datapad. Some
of the names he didn't recognize, but many he did.
They were among the most illustrious and revered
members.

He had no illusions about corruption in the Senate.
But he was shocked to find that so many Senators
would be involved in an illegal scheme such as this
one. Among the names was Bail Organa, the Senator
from Alderaan Obi-Wan had always respected for his in-
tegrity. Why would someone like Organa risk his career
in order to make a few credits on a bet?

The bets had to be substantial, he supposed.

Or else the Senators have no fear that they'll be caught.

He had to deal with Anakin, but he had to pursue this first. Obi-Wan found Bog in a VIP box watching a match of krovation. When Astri saw him, her smile was wide and welcoming.

"Obi-Wan! How good of you to come by. The match is almost finished."

Obi-Wan looked at the two teams vying with poles on the field. "As much as I like krovatin, I have to decline. I'm here on business. I need to speak with Bog."

Astri's smile dimmed at the look on his face. She frowned and stepped aside. "Please join us."

Obi-Wan walked into the box. Bog fastened the jeweled clasp to his dark red septsilk robe as the Jedi approached.

"How can I help you, Obi-Wan?"

Obi-Wan hesitated, his hand on the datapad in his inner pocket. "If you prefer to speak alone . . ."

Bog smiled. "I hide nothing from Astri."

His smile showed not a trace of worry, but Astri walked to his side. Her eyes were grave now. Astri was perceptive, and she knew Obi-Wan well. "What is it, Obi-Wan?"

Obi-Wan withdrew the datapad. "I have something of yours."

Bog hurried forward. "You found it? Where? Thank you!"

Obi-Wan sidestepped the question of where he had found it. He slipped the datapad back into his pocket. "I'm afraid I can't return it just yet. I must confess that I took a look at your files, Bog."

Bog looked disconcerted. "Well, I see. I suppose that is all right. I have no secrets."

Obi-Wan was puzzled. Bog did not seem guilty or worried. "I accessed the file referring to the work you've done for the Senators."

"Yes, I arranged special seating for them," Bog said, nodding. "Is there a problem with some of the skyboxes?" He looked puzzled. "I didn't know Jedi cared about such things."

"We don't," Obi-Wan said quietly. "But you did not arrange skyboxes for the Senators. You placed bets for them on events in which the outcome is assured. This is not only illegal, but it has the potential to spark conflict among the member worlds."

"Obi-Wan, I don't know what you're talking about," Bog interrupted, shaking his head. "The Games are fixed? Senators betting? I can't believe that. All I did was place orders for special seating. You must be mistaken."

Obi-Wan studied Bog as the crowd around them

roared at a player's score. "If you are not involved, you are being used. Where did you get the instructions on how to proceed? How did you know which Senators to find seating for?"

"Liviani gave me the list of Senators," Bog said. "That is standard. The head of the Games Council always gets a list of important beings throughout the galaxy to accord special favors to. I used the Council funds to pay the Ruling Power for the skyboxes. You see, the Ruling Power makes the seating available. They have all the stadium plans. Arranging seating may seem trivial, but it's a very important task."

"So who did you contact to arrange the skyboxes?"

"As it turned out, I didn't have to contact anyone. He came to me. An odd four-eyed creature. His name was Boosa . . . no, that's not it. Beesa . . ."

"Besum?"

"That's it." Bog nodded as the crowd jeered a questionable play. "I transferred the credits and ordered the seating from Boosa . . . ah, Besum, and he handed me the receipts."

"Do you have them?"

"No. I placed them in the welcome packs for the Senators." At last the seriousness of the matter began to penetrate Bog's self-absorption. "I only followed protocol," he said nervously.

Obi-Wan frowned. Why would the Senators want receipts to be placed in their welcome packets? Anyone could see them. He would think they would go to great lengths to hide the fact that they were betting on the Games.

Could it be that the Senators themselves don't know about this?

Could it be that the Ruling Power has arranged this in order to disgrace them?

But why?

Bog grew restless at Obi-Wan's silence. "I didn't place any bets! I'm sure this is a misunderstanding."

"I'm sure it isn't," Astri said to her husband. "Obi-Wan knows what he's talking about." She turned to Obi-Wan. "Is Bog in trouble?"

Bog swallowed. "If I am, I will face it."

"*We* will face it," Astri said, putting her hand on Bog's arm. "Together."

Obi-Wan saw the look that Bog gave Astri, a look of tenderness and devotion. He saw that Bog did love Astri, and his instincts told him that Bog had been used as a pawn in the scheme. No doubt whoever was behind it did not care if Bog took the fall.

Looking at the love on Astri's face for her husband, Obi-Wan decided that he would do anything in his power to make sure that did not happen. He remembered a time long ago when Astri had cut off her pretty curls, shaved her head, and learned how to shoot a blaster in order to help him track down Qui-Gon. She had not thought of herself as a brave person, but she had faced down blaster bolts and a laser whip, and had never left his side. No, he would not let anything happen to Astri.

"Bog will not be in trouble if he didn't do anything wrong," Obi-Wan told the couple. "I will make sure of that. Now, please excuse me."

Obi-Wan stepped outside, leaving the sounds of the match behind him. He quickly contacted Jocasta Nu at the Temple.

"I am sending you a list of Senators. I need to know if there is any link among them." Obi-Wan waited for her to read the list of names. "Does anything come to mind right now?" he asked.

"Nothing," Jocasta Nu said. "There are many ways Senators can be linked, Obi-Wan. Through sponsoring legislation. Committees. Subcommittees. Special hearings. Oversight subcommittees on special hearings —"

"I get the picture," Obi-Wan said. "Just do the best you can, as quickly as you can. Can you also look into the Ruling Power, and see if there is some connection with those Senators?"

"Of course. I'll contact you as soon as I have information."

Obi-Wan thanked Jocasta Nu and cut the communication. He leaned against the railing and looked out over the sprawling city. Beings streamed through the streets, and he could hear the distant roar of a crowd in the nearby stadium. If the betting were exposed, the Senators involved would be drawn into a scandal. It would not matter if they were guilty or innocent. Their reputations would suffer. Was that the goal?

An insider, Fligh had said. It could be someone in the Ruling Power. Or someone close to the Games themselves.

He called up Bog's file on his datapad again. He flipped through the holographic files, remembering the notations on Uso Yso's screen.

The bets had been placed on the bowcaster skill contest, the obstacle course race, and the Podrace. The same events that Aarno Dering had on his datapad.

Obi-Wan contacted Didi on his comlink. "Have you found out where Fligh is staying?"

"The Sleek Cruiser Inn on Grand Eucer Street," Didi said. "Room 2222. But let me assure you, my friend, this inn is no sleek cruiser. More like a garbage barge."

"Just make sure Fligh doesn't go off-planet," Obi-Wan told Didi. "Contact me if he does."

"I am your servant, Obi-Wan."

Obi-Wan tapped his finger on his comlink, planning his next move. He could handle Fligh, but on the other hand, this was more than a pesky problem. It was time to call in the other Jedi teams.

He activated his comlink and contacted Siri. He filled her in on what he had discovered.

"It seems as though the Ruling Power could be behind this," he said. "They might want to blackmail Senators in order to gain power in the Senate, getting appointed to powerful posts. But we have no real proof, and we don't have much time. All three events are scheduled to take place this afternoon."

"What do you need?" Siri asked, getting to the point as quickly as possible, as she usually did.

"I have to pay a visit to Fligh, and I'd like some company," Obi-Wan said. "I think some additional Jedi presence is needed."

"I'll be there. And I'll contact Ry-Gaul," Siri said.

The problem of Anakin entering the Podrace had never left Obi-Wan's mind. Why had his Padawan done such a thing without telling him? It was not the first time Anakin's impulsiveness had worried and alarmed Obi-Wan.

His comlink signaled. Anakin was calling. Obi-Wan answered.

"Master, things have developed here," Anakin said.

"Sebulba has recognized me. Because of that, Deland stepped in to avoid a fight and was injured. He cannot race. I . . . I offered to race in his place. Doby and Deland are trying to free their sister —"

"And is that your mission on Euceron, to free Djulla?" Obi-Wan asked sternly.

"No," Anakin said. "But was it Qui-Gon's mission to free me? Must we follow a mission so exactly that we turn our backs on beings who need help? *Every mission has a detour.* You've told me that."

"I've also told you that it is the mark of a Jedi to recognize whether or not to follow the detour," Obi-Wan reminded him.

"Then I ask you to let me make this choice," Anakin replied.

His Padawan's voice was firm. There was no pleading, no uncertainty. He wanted what he wanted. Was that the right thing in this circumstance?

Obi-Wan pondered the problem. "Have you learned anything else?" he asked.

"The Podrace is scheduled to take place this afternoon at three. A viewing area has been set up for spectators in the underground caves. Sebulba has placed enormous bets on his son to win. The official timekeeper is supposed to send the Podrace route directly to onboard computers. But I don't know who will take over the job now that Dering is dead. I think the best way I can find out how the race is fixed and who is behind it is to enter it myself."

"All right," Obi-Wan said reluctantly. He did not like the sound of pleasure in Anakin's voice. He would ask Siri and Ry-Gaul to send Ferus and Tru to observe while Anakin piloted the Podracer. He could not be there with his Padawan, but he did not want Anakin to be alone.

CHAPTER FIFTEEN

"I got it!" Anakin crowed. He tweaked the last screw to the energy-binder plate. "We're set."

"Whew," Doby said, pushing his goggles to the top of his head. Two round circles of grime circled his eyes. "I was getting worried."

"Maybe I should give the computer system another check," Anakin wondered.

"I did it," Deland said. "You've done enough, Anakin. I actually think we're ready." He patted the Pod-racer with his good hand. His other arm was encased in a rigid bandage from elbow to fingers.

Anakin jumped off the scaffold he'd used to work on the turbines. "I know I am."

Suddenly, his smile dimmed. He spied Ferus and

Tru threading their way toward him through a sea of pit droids and mechanics and pilots, the usual frenzy of a pit hangar before a race.

My Master sent them. He doesn't trust me. The thought seared Anakin's mind before rationality set in. It would be helpful to have backup, he told himself, trying to be logical. There was nothing wrong with that. He dodged a lubricant hose and went forward to meet them.

Tru's head swiveled, taking in the excitement. "Strange, if you think about it," he said to Anakin.

Anakin wiped his hands on a rag. "What?"

"That Podraces are so dangerous, but nobody looks scared," he said.

"There are beings who equate danger with pleasure," Ferus said, his eyes dark with disapproval. "It is a mistake easily made for those who do not think deeply." He gave Anakin a cool look.

"Well, there's such a thing as fun, Ferus," Tru said amiably. "Even you have to admit that."

"Yes," Ferus said. "But not here." His cool gaze did not falter as he studied Anakin. "I'm not clear on why you are racing, Anakin."

"It is the best way to discover how the race is fixed," Anakin said.

Ferus shifted his gaze to take in Doby and Deland and the Podracer, then scanned the rest of the hangar. "I see. Our Masters have told us that it is possible that advance knowledge of the track will be sent to one Podracer's nav computer seconds before it is given to the rest. Do you know which Podracer that is?"

"Hekula," Anakin said. "The Dug. The third Podracer down on the left."

"You know this for sure?"

"It is a guess," Anakin admitted. "Based on my knowledge of him."

Ferus turned back. "And that is all?"

"Sebulba, his father, proposed the new rule," Anakin said. "Sebulba never proposes anything unless he knows he can profit by it."

"Do you know when and how the information will be transmitted to the nav computers?"

"At the start of the race, and then at three-minute intervals," Anakin said.

"So how do you propose to beat him?" Ferus asked.

"By being faster and better," Anakin answered. "I have something he doesn't have. I have the Force."

"Who is the timekeeper?" Tru asked. "Do you think he is the one who will transmit the information?"

Anakin nodded. "A race referee. The computer system is already in place. Dering has already designed the program. This person will just follow instructions."

Ferus frowned. "Isn't there any way to tell whoever is in charge of the race what is going on? Surely it would be better to simply cancel the race. Did you think of that?"

Anakin's cheeks flushed. Ferus was questioning every detail of what he had learned as though he were a Jedi Master and Anakin was his Padawan.

"I'm sure Anakin thought of it," Tru said. "But we can't be sure who knows that the program is a cheat. Whoever it is could alter it with a keystroke and we'd never know who was behind it, or why."

"Maybe there is still some way to find out," Ferus said. "Tru and I will investigate." He glanced at the Podracer. "You can go back to your energy-binder plate."

Tru hung back as Ferus walked off. "He's just being careful," he told Anakin.

Anakin's teeth gritted. "Is that what you call it?"

"You'll understand him one day," Tru said. "After you become friends."

"I will never be friends with Ferus Olin," Anakin answered savagely.

Tru studied him for a moment. "I feel . . . some darkness from you, Anakin. Your enemy is here. But Sebulba cannot hurt you anymore. Remember, Jedi do not have enemies."

"I just want to win," Anakin said.

"You mean you want to prevent injury and ensure fairness," Tru corrected.

Anakin nodded. "That too."

CHAPTER SIXTEEN

The Sleek Cruiser Inn was just as Didi had described it, a dilapidated building made of patchwork plasteel sheeting. Seeing a way to rake in more credits, the owner had leased out space in the hallways and closets. Travelers from around the galaxy had stashed gear in every spare space and were cooking up meals on portable stoves in the hallways. Others had rolled themselves in bedrolls in various corners and were trying to catch a nap between events. The smell of bodies, food, and dust was overwhelming. Even this far from the Games, the hum of the crowds in the arenas could be heard. Obi-Wan, Siri, and Ry-Gaul picked through the mess and knocked on Fligh's door.

"I said I would settle the bill on the way out!" Fligh yelled behind the door. "Such a hospitable establishment, I can't wait to return!" He flung the door open and saw the Jedi. He swallowed. "Ah, Jedi. Always a good sign."

He stepped aside and let them enter. Belongings were stuffed into an open case. Still-wet laundry spilled out of a travel pack. A half-eaten meal was spread on the sleep couch. It was clear that Fligh was in the midst of a hasty departure.

"Leaving so soon?" Obi-Wan asked. "The Games have just begun."

"I'm not a fan," Fligh said, shrugging. "There you go."

"Yet you came here to see the Games," Obi-Wan pointed out. "Don't you want to see how your bets turn out?"

Fligh laughed. "Why? You have made sure I don't win. I may as well return to Coruscant and make my living honestly, as a thief."

Siri and Ry-Gaul closed the door and stood in front of it. Obi-Wan casually flung one leg over a stool and sat. "A funny thing happened after we left you this morning. We took an air taxi —"

"Always a good idea," Fligh said nervously. "The streets are so crowded."

"— and the pilot tried to crash it," Obi-Wan went on. "Odd that he knew just where we were and where we were headed."

"Maybe you were just lucky."

"Maybe you'd like to accompany us to the security office of the Ruling Power and talk about it," Obi-Wan said. It was a bluff. He did not want the Ruling Power to know that they were investigating.

Fligh gave a squeak of disappointment and threw himself down on the unmade sleep couch. "I knew I'd never make it off this blasted planet. All right. When you came to ask me about the fixed events, you made me nervous. Why wouldn't I be? I saw my fortune disappearing in front of my eyes. So I might have alerted someone as to your presence. They weren't supposed to kill you. Just delay you. I swear! Didi is my friend. I would never allow harm to come to him. And if you think I'd tangle with Jedi, you underestimate my cowardice."

"Yet you lie to us," Obi-Wan said.

"And that is never a good idea," Siri said.

Ry-Gaul did not have to say a word. His fierce looks spoke for him.

"Yes, I see what you mean," Fligh said, backing away on the sleep couch.

"Now, tell me again about your friend Quentor," Obi-Wan said, leaning forward.

"Ha ha," Fligh said. "I see you know about my little joke. I thought it better to protect a friend than expose him."

"Who?" Obi-Wan asked softly. "And tell me the truth this time."

"Aarno Dering," Fligh said. "Weeks ago, I was contacted anonymously. Through messages on my datapad. I was asked to find someone who could rig a false timing device for a major race. Credits were transferred into my account with a promise of a sure bet to come. I happened to know just the person they needed. Aarno had been the timekeeper for races in the Outer Rim. He was known for a certain . . . uh, casualness when it came to scorekeeping. Then the anonymous person said they would hire Aarno for the Galactic Games. The Galactic Games! I had no idea it was for something so grand."

"How could he pass scrutiny?" Siri wondered. "The timers and judges are screened very closely."

"That was just my question," Fligh said, nodding. "They told me not to worry about it. To my great surprise, Aarno was hired for several events. To Aarno's surprise as well."

"That's why you concluded that an insider had to be involved," Obi-Wan said.

Fligh nodded. "Who else could get Aarno hired, with his record? So we came to Euceron and Aarno got his instructions. It seemed like a deal as sweet as a piece of blumfruit. Aarno would find a way to shave a few seconds here and there and we'd take off with a small fortune. I didn't expect anyone to get hurt. Didi was almost killed, and Aarno got run over by a speeder." Fligh shivered. "I'm going back to Coruscant, where I'll be safe. I just paved the way for some bets to be placed. I didn't want anyone to get killed."

"You got the false text docs for Dering," Obi-Wan guessed. "Why did he suddenly want to get off-planet?"

"I guess he lost his nerve," Fligh said with a nervous glance at Ry-Gaul.

Siri had moved so that she was now sitting in front of Fligh on her haunches, her hands dangling. Her bright blue gaze was piercing. "There is something you're not telling us. Why was Aarno so afraid?"

Fligh fingered one of his long ears. "I had an appointment to drop the text docs off to Aarno right after the swoop race. As soon as you left, I went to his quarters and waited for him. He was in a big hurry to leave Euceron, and I asked him why. He said if I knew what was good for me, I'd leave too. Of course, I had to pressure him. I withheld the text docs until he told me. He thought he had been hired just to fix the events. But then he found out something else. Something's going to happen during an event. Something will go wrong. They want people to get killed during an event so that the Senators will be blamed."

"Which event?" Obi-Wan asked.

"I don't know," Fligh admitted. "Aarno didn't tell me. He found out by mistake. He was afraid they would come after him because he knew."

"Who are *they*?" Siri barked in frustration.

"I didn't ask," Fligh said with a shudder. "I don't want to know. I'm in over my head. And if I know anything about anything — which I don't, but I know about this — sooner or later it's going to occur to them that I know too much. And it's going to be sooner, not later. All in all I'd rather be on Coruscant, so if you don't mind —"

Obi-Wan, Siri, and Ry-Gaul turned toward the door at the same instant. The surge in the Force had warned them. At the same time, the sound of heavy rolling could be heard in the corridor outside Fligh's room.

"Hey, I'm over here, guys," Fligh said. "Are you going to answer my quest —"

Before Fligh could finish the word, the door blasted apart and a squad of droidekas appeared in the smoldering opening.

CHAPTER SEVENTEEN

Fligh dived behind the sleep couch as the Jedi ignited their lightsabers. The droidekas unfurled and snapped into attack position, blaster bolts firing. Obi-Wan's lightsaber was an arc of moving light, deflecting the shower of blaster fire. Beside him Siri's lightsaber swung in a continuous arc of precise movement, with Siri's two-handed grip and her graceful footwork. Ry-Gaul did not move. He did not need to. His long arms were a blur in the air as his lightsaber shifted from hand to hand.

The three-legged droidekas were built for battle and close to invincible — but these droidekas weren't shielded. Their heavy armor shells and volts of firepower as well as their maneuverability made them capable of cutting down opponents with fearsome efficiency.

It wasn't as though their power alarmed Obi-Wan. But he still was not especially pleased to see them. There were twelve of them, so he was glad to have Ry-Gaul and Siri by his side.

The air filled with smoke as the blaster bolts zinged, but the Jedi deflected them and struck blow after blow at the heavy armor plates on the droids. Because the doorway was narrow, the droidekas began firing through the wall itself, quickly tearing gaping holes in the structure. After a sweep from Siri's lightsaber, one droideka smoked and fell, and another, its legs gone, bobbled and spun until it crashed against a wall. Obi-Wan sliced a droideka in two and sent one piece flying over the sleep couch and crashing into the wall. Fligh shrieked as pieces of hot metal rained down on him.

Droidekas had control centers, not brains. They could not feel fear or apprehension. The amazing skill of the Jedi was lost on them. They continued to advance and fire, continued to evade by rolling themselves into balls and repositioning themselves to fire again. Time after time they attacked, and time after time the Jedi struck blow after blow until the harsh smoke and the heat caused Fligh to have a coughing fit. The Jedi did not react to the smoke. Their minds and bodies were focused on battle, and nothing else mattered but the moment.

Suddenly all three Jedi exchanged a glance. They

leaped back as the flimsy wall collapsed on the remaining droidekas. Ry-Gaul, Obi-Wan, and Siri finished the rest off, disabling them with lightsaber thrusts. At last the droidekas lay around them in pieces. Fligh raised his head from behind the sleep couch.

His voice was hoarse. "Can I go now?"

"He can't help us," Obi-Wan told the others. "He's told us everything he knows." He deactivated his lightsaber. "Yes, Fligh. You can go."

"Until next time, Obi-Wan," Fligh said fervently.

"I certainly hope not," Obi-Wan answered. Wherever Fligh was, trouble was soon to follow.

With a last bow, Fligh ran from the room, his belongings trailing from his packing case.

"If they're sending Destroyer Droids, they must be worried," Siri said. "Whoever *they* are."

"One of us should attend each event," Obi-Wan said. "The Padawans are already at the Podrace and it's scheduled to begin in . . . fifteen minutes. Can you head out there, Ry-Gaul? I'll contact Anakin and tell him that something is supposed to go wrong, but I'd feel better if you were there."

Ry-Gaul gave a short nod and left the room, stepping over a pile of droidekas in the doorway.

"I'll take the bowcaster skill contest," Siri said. "It's at Stadium Seven."

"That leaves me with the obstacle course," Obi-Wan said, nodding. "Stay in touch."

"I just wish I knew what I was looking for," Siri said.

Obi-Wan tucked his lightsaber into his belt. "That makes two of us."

Obi-Wan was able to give Anakin an update on the way to Stadium Nine. There was nothing much for Anakin to do except what the rest of them were doing — being mindful, and watching.

Obi-Wan strode into the stadium. He felt the heat and the noise of a crowd eager for the event to begin.

As the Euceron hero and record-setter for the event in the last Galactic Games, Maxo Vista was here as well. Obi-Wan found a seat as close to the judges as he could and watched on a viewscreen overhead while Vista's podium zoomed to the center of the stadium.

"Welcome, all," he said, his voice amplified throughout the stadium. "I'd like to introduce myself. I am —"

"MAXO VISTA!" the crowd roared.

"You may not remember me —"

The crowd roared once again.

"— but I was at this event seven years ago —"

A cheer went up.

"— I didn't do too badly —" Vista paused and waited for the cheers and laughter "— and I truly hope that today, my record will be broken. I'm just a Galactic Games official now, seven years older and seven years slower, so I'd better make way for the next generation of athletes."

The broad grin still on his face, Vista suddenly vaulted off the platform. The crowd gasped, but a cable launcher hidden in Vista's belt let out a long line, and he bounced at the end of it, only centimeters away from the ground. With a powerful thrust, he flipped his body upward, then twisted, flew through the air, and landed on his feet. His movements were so graceful it was more like a dance than an athletic feat.

The crowd erupted in cheers and applause. The cheers went on and on.

The cheers fell away for Obi-Wan. He heard only the absence of sound, the silence of concentration and revelation.

The lines of Vista's body were suddenly familiar, the fluid, powerful way he moved. The way he made something that took great effort look effortless.

Maxo Vista was the air-taxi pilot who had tried to kill them. And he was the speeder driver who had run down Aarno Dering.

Which meant that the great hero of Euceron was the insider who was behind fixing the Games.

CHAPTER EIGHTEEN

It was his fault. If he hadn't been so irritated at *not* knowing who Maxo Vista was, he would have looked closer at him. He had made a mistake worthy of a Jedi Temple student, not an experienced Jedi Knight. He had allowed his own perspective, his own emotion, to color his perception.

Perception comes from not one but all angles at once.

Yes, Qui-Gon.

Obi-Wan raced down the moving walkway that circled the stadium. He had to make it down to Level Twenty, where Maxo Vista would enter the VIP box. He could not risk losing Maxo Vista the way he had lost Aarno Dering.

He was almost at the door of the box when Astri

dashed toward him, curls bouncing and robe swirling. "Obi-Wan!"

"Later," he said tersely, striding toward the door.

She grabbed his arm. "You must know this! The Podrace! Something terrible is going to happen!"

He half-turned and searched her dark eyes. "How do you know this?"

"Bog," she said. "He went to Maxo Vista to tell him what you had discovered —"

Obi-Wan almost groaned aloud.

"— Vista wasn't there, and so Bog accessed his datapad. He thought as a fellow Council member he could do this —" Her hand to her throat, Astri got the words out fast, between her panting breaths. "— and discovered that the Podrace is not only fixed, but booby-trapped. The nav computer will lead the Podracers close to the city's hub. The lead Podracer will get taken over by the nav computer. It will be made to crash into the crowd! We don't know if Vista himself is aware of this, it could have been sent to his dataport without his knowing. We cannot believe that Maxo Vista would be involved. Bog replaced the datapad and told me what he'd seen. He is going to tell Liviani Sarno. But I came to you."

"Does Vista know about this?" *Anakin is in danger.* Obi-Wan reached for his comlink as he asked the question.

"I didn't. But now I do." Vista's voice came from behind him. He smiled as Obi-Wan turned. "I promise you, I can explain everything. This way, Obi-Wan."

Obi-Wan hesitated.

"Trust me." Maxo Vista had a blaster pointed at Astri, but the friendly grin was still on his face. Astri could not see the blaster, which was on his other side.

"This way," he repeated meaningfully to Obi-Wan.

Obi-Wan stepped inside. He would follow Maxo Vista's instructions, but only for a few seconds. He had to make sure Vista would not hit anyone with blaster fire.

The floor moved under his feet. He realized that he had not stepped out into the VIP box, but onto a moving podium. It suddenly zoomed to the center of the stadium. Vista's hand dropped and the blaster was lost in the folds of his cloak.

"It is a long-range model, and it is still pointed at Astri," he said pleasantly.

Obi-Wan tried to signal Astri to move, but she stood watching him from afar, not knowing the blaster was pointed at her. He could reach for his lightsaber, but he wasn't sure if even he could be fast enough to block the shot.

Light suddenly hit his eyes, dazzling him for a moment. "Welcome to the exhibition match!" Maxo Vista's voice was amplified throughout the stadium. "Jedi against athlete! Let the event begin!"

The crowd roared. A cube of white light settled over Obi-Wan. Another flashed over Maxo Vista. A holographic image of a treton, a wild creature from the planet Aesolian, appeared in front of them. On the tip of one pointed ear a green laser glowed. His snarl was amplified and echoed through the stadium. There was a collective *ooooohh* of fear. Even though the spectators knew the treton was holographic, its fierce battle cry struck terror into their hearts.

An announcer's steady voice boomed over the stadium. "Ten seconds. Contestants, prepare. . . ."

Obi-Wan reached for his comlink to contact Anakin, but it was dead. Now he remembered that in the stadium center a jamming device was employed so that no contestants could use hidden devices to aid them in their events. Maxo Vista had trapped him, no doubt in order to buy time.

Obi-Wan judged the distance back to the stadium. It was too far. The podium was too high for even a cable launcher. He would have to wait. He was now officially in the obstacle course, and subject to its rules. He was trapped. And Anakin was just about to begin the Podrace.

"Welcome to my world, Obi-Wan Kenobi," Maxo

Vista whispered. "I had a feeling the Jedi would show up, so I've been planning this. Sorry it had to be this way, but at least you'll have some fun before you die."

"Five seconds, contestants . . ."

A lightweight weapon emerged out of the platform floor in front of Obi-Wan. He grabbed it. At the tip was a green laser. Obi-Wan guessed that in order to score points, he would have to hit the laser on the hologram with the laser tip of his weapon. He wished he had seen a holographic obstacle course before. He had no idea what was in store.

"Yes, Obi-Wan. Something will go wrong and you will die in this stadium. You won't know when it will come, or how to fight it." Maxo Vista smiled. "May the best man win. Which means me, of course."

"Begin!" the announcer said.

The treton rushed forward. Maxo Vista was pre- pared. He charged ahead and slashed at the Treton even as it zoomed upward and around in a crazy eva- sive dance that no bulky treton would ever accomplish. Vista hit the creature precisely on the ear and a loud joyful *clang clang!* resounded through the stadium.

"Point, Vista," the voice announced. The stadium erupted in cheers for the favorite.

Obi-Wan's laser tip now glowed pink. The edge of

the platform elongated into a ramp that rose almost straight upward. Vista began to bound ahead.

After a second of hesitation, Obi-Wan followed. He had no choice. He would have to hope that somewhere in the course he would be able to break free.

Obi-Wan gained on Vista easily. At the top of the ramp six snarling holographic neks sat guard. At the center of their collars, a laser glowed like a pink jewel.

Now Obi-Wan knew that he had to hit each of the creatures precisely with the tip of his weapon, laser to laser, in order to progress.

Vista sprang forward as the nek on the far left lunged, teeth bared. Vista twisted, but the holographic teeth grazed his ankle. A harsh buzzer sounded.

"Minus point five," the announcer said.

Obi-Wan somersaulted, avoiding the two neks who flew at him. He used the weapon like a lightsaber, touching the collars lightly. Two loud *clang clang! clang clang!* noises sounded, and he whirled and touched the other collars just as delicately, even as Vista was moving toward them. *Clang clang!* The neks dissolved in a shower of light.

"Six points, Visitor." This time the cheers were not nearly as deafening.

The laser shifted to blue. Ahead was a cliff face with

shallow ledges forming a pathway upward. At the top were three multi-clawed ravenscreechers, large birds from the Outer Rim planet Wxtm. Each had a large wing span and six legs with claws half a meter long. Instead of an eye, a bright blue laser spot winked at Obi-Wan from each bird.

Vista hurled himself at the cliff and began to climb. Obi-Wan followed. Vista reached out a leg and tried to kick him. The crowd hissed disapproval. No doubt Vista was risking the displeasure of the crowd in order to vent his anger at Obi-Wan defeating all the neks.

Yes, you are a record-holder, Obi-Wan thought. *But you've never competed against a Jedi.*

Accessing the Force, he vaulted into the air, bypassing Vista and landing on a ledge close to the edge. The ravenscreechers took off, diving toward him.

While the crowd roared and cheered, Obi-Wan held on with only one hand. He slashed at one holographic bird, touching its eye and gaining a point, then hit the next one on a backswing without even turning. Using the momentum, he swung himself up to the top of the cliff and hit the third one as it rose to attack him.

Clang clang! The points rang up on the screen. His laser tip flashed yellow. Now more of the crowd was on his side, and Maxo Vista was furious. His face was bright red as he scrambled from ledge to ledge, racing to catch Obi-Wan.

On top of the ledge sat two swoops. Obi-Wan was about to spring forward when a tentacle bush appeared, its branches reaching out for him. It took him a moment to locate the tiny glowing tip of the yellow laser in the heart of the bush. If one of the other branches hit him, he would lose points.

He could feel Vista behind him and was not surprised when the man launched himself at the bush. He knew Vista was furious, and anger would make him careless. He would give Vista the first chance at the bush, but he would not allow him to beat him to the swoops.

The branches moved like the arms of dancers, fluid and graceful, yet lethal in their striking motions. In his fury, Vista tried to attack the bush with stabbing motions, but the waving branches kept him just out of reach. His movements were as fluid as that of the branches, and the crowd began to chant his name.

Obi-Wan leaped. He somersaulted in midair, keeping his legs tucked close to his body to avoid the waving branches. When he was dead center over the bush, he reached down amid the cluster of wildly waving branches and touched the glowing laser with his weapon. Then he landed precisely on one of the swoops, legs astride, and took off. The whole operation had taken less than three seconds.

The crowd was stunned into silence. The noise of the announcer echoed through the nearly silent stadium.

"Point, Visitor."

The crowd went wild.

Obi-Wan did not think about what was behind him. Only what was ahead. The minutes were ticking away, and he had to contact Anakin. The worry ticked away inside him, but his movements did not betray him. Vista's warning that something would occur on the course didn't worry him. He trusted in the Force to warn him.

Ahead were glowing circles of light. Holographic humming peepers twittered overhead. Each held a tiny violet laser in its beak. Obi-Wan saw that he would have to navigate through the spinning circles without touching the edges of each one, hitting as many humming peepers as he could. This obstacle did not require strength, but agility and precision.

He did not look behind him, but he knew Maxo Vista was pushing his swoop to maximum speed. Obi-Wan only saw the glowing obstacles and the tiny birds. He dived through the first hoop and delicately touched the tiny bird with his weapon. The clanging noise sounded, then sounded again a second later. Vista, too, had scored a point.

Vista piloted the swoop as if it were part of his body. He leaned over and scored another point, then flipped the swoop to quickly zoom through a circle. The crowd kept up a steady roar now. Vista pushed his swoop, aiming for the back of Obi-Wan's. He bumped Obi-Wan's swoop but it appeared he was only attempting to get through the next loop. Obi-Wan knew better. He dived, engines screaming, then came at the next loop from an extreme right angle. He zoomed through the loop with a centimeter to spare. Taken off guard, Maxo Vista brushed against the side of the loop and lost five points.

Obi-Wan zigzagged through the air of the stadium, sailing through the loops and hitting the laser targets. Vista gave up trying to unseat him and concentrated on gaining points. Soon the humming peepers had all been hit. The glowing hoops dissolved into particles of light.

The stadium went black. Obi-Wan immediately pulled back on the swoop's power and hovered in the air, waiting. Below, on the mid-level landing platform, a group of holographic Gladiator Droids appeared. Bright orange erupted from flame projectors in their fists. A bright red laser winked in the center of their foreheads.

Obi-Wan flew down to the landing platform and

leaped off the swoop. The Gladiator Droids shot blaster fire at him, just harmless points of light. The flames licked close to him but there was no heat. He could not use the race weapon or his lightsaber against light, so he had to dodge the flames and blaster bolts.

This obstacle was similar to an exercise called Art of Movement at the Temple, introduced to him when he was just a student, even younger than Anakin. The students were required to keep moving, dodging both lines of light that zigzagged the room and points that scampered randomly. The objective was simply to get from the door to the opposite wall. The exercise required split-second timing and an agile body. Some students were better than others at compressing their limbs, jumping, and flattening themselves against the floor. As a human, Obi-Wan was hampered by his solid skeletal frame, but he had practiced for hours until he could judge the best way to move with a minimum of effort. He had even had private tutorials with the Jedi Knight Fy-Tor-Ana, known for her grace.

All of the lessons came back to him in a rush. He had not trained for this specifically, as Maxo Vista had. He hadn't practiced the Art of Movement in years. But he could feel his body respond and move even as the laser points skittered around him. Using the Force, he was able to gauge where the pinpoints of light would hit.

Maxo Vista had trained for this. He was adept at movement. The crowd gasped at the flexible grace of the two opponents. Obi-Wan got close enough to one Gladiator Droid to score a point. Vista scored another. In the dim light, the shimmering outlines of the Droids melted against the velvet darkness.

Obi-Wan could feel the Force around him and feel the ripples of disturbance. Maxo Vista's surprise was near. Even as he dodged the light and moved in to strike another blow at a Gladiator Droid, he knew what was coming.

One of the Droids was real.

Obi-Wan had to use the Force. It was too dark to be absolutely sure. The lights exploding around him could be lethal or not. He noted now that Maxo Vista was pretending to be slow, keeping Obi-Wan between him and the fire.

He saw a Gladiator Droid well behind the others, its blasters firing. That was the one.

He unsheathed his lightsaber. With his lightsaber in one hand and his event weapon in the other, he leaped. With one hand, he hit each laser target on each droid, twisting and hanging in midair. With the other, he deflected the real blaster fire.

He ended with a midair somersault and sank his lightsaber into the real droid's control panel.

The counter rang furiously. The scoreboard lit up. The crowd was on its feet now, stamping its approval.

The lights in the stadium came up. Maxo Vista raised his head from his position crouching on the floor. He blinked, surprised to hear the boos directed at him.

The crowd screamed for the Jedi. But Obi-Wan had disappeared.

CHAPTER NINETEEN

Doby and Deland paced nervously by the Podracer. "Maybe we should check the intake valves again," Doby said.

"We've checked them three times," Anakin said. "Everything is fine. We're ready to go."

He was strapped into his seat, his goggles pushed up on his head. The official starter stood talking to the Podrace organizer. Hekula was receiving last-minute instructions from Sebulba.

It all felt so familiar. He could be back in the Mos Espa Grand Arena again. His mother was watching. Qui-Gon and Padmé were there. He wanted to do his best for them.

Anakin swallowed against the emotion that swelled in him. He was older now. Things were more complicated. His emotions would never be so simple again. But here in the cockpit doubt fell away and uncertainty had no place. Left behind was only one goal: winning.

"All right, then," Deland said. He held his arm carefully against his side, and his face was pale. "Good luck, Anakin. We won't forget this. Neither will Djulla."

"We shouldn't have let you, but we had to." Doby leaned in to speak to him earnestly. "Don't worry. You're going to win. Just don't crash."

Anakin grinned. "Right."

"Come on, Doby, you're making him nervous." Deland yanked his brother away.

Ry-Gaul approached Anakin. He stood by the Podracer, his gray eyes scanning the spectators who had gathered on the stands near the finish line. "You must use the Force to stay ahead. There is darkness here, but I cannot locate it."

It was the longest speech Anakin had ever heard Ry-Gaul give. Anakin nodded. "I feel it, too." But along with the darkness, he felt the excitement of the race to come.

Tru waved at him from the sidelines. Anakin gave him a thumbs-up, just as he had to his best friend Kitster so many years ago.

"Start your engines," the race official called.

Anakin engaged his engines. They roared to life.

Ry-Gaul's mouth moved, but he couldn't hear the words. It didn't matter. He knew what Ry-Gaul had said.

May the Force be with you.

The noise of the powerful engines of eight Podracers was deafening. It bounced off the high cave walls. The floor shook like a groundquake. Besides himself, Hekula, and Aldar Beedo, Anakin recognized Gasgano, Elan Mak, and Ody Mandrell. The last two Podracers were Scorch Zanales, a Daimlo, and Will Neluenf, heir to the first great Tatooine Podracer, Ben Neluenf.

Anakin felt the power of the engines under his hands. He felt warm and liquid, alert and calm. His senses were hyperaware. The shimmer of the air, the dull red of the cave walls, the smell of the fuel — it filled his head and sharpened his focus. He was ready.

He kept his eye on the starting light. It turned from red to yellow . . .

Green! Anakin pushed the throttle and the engines roared in response. He had always believed in a quick start. His old Podracer had been tweaked to allow for maximum fuel flow. Deland's Podracer surged forward in a pack with the others, but slightly ahead. He allowed himself one glance over at Hekula. Sebulba's son bared his teeth at Anakin.

Anakin checked the nav computer. In a glance he saw the route ahead. Down a long underground canyon, then through a series of dips and rolls. Then he needed to take a sharp left down a narrow passage. After that he would receive the next stage of the course.

The cave walls were a blur of dusty red and the screaming engines were just a backdrop of constant sound as Anakin raced through the canyon. Hekula pulled ahead, the double engines of Anakin's old pod bobbing on the air current created by his speed. Anakin stayed close on Hekula's tail, avoiding the flying engines. The other Podracers were reluctant to get too close. Anakin knew from experience how the engines would move as Hekula maneuvered. He dared to race snug against the back of Hekula's Podracer, knowing he was making Hekula angry and nervous.

The dips were ahead. Anakin pulled back suddenly, and Hekula shot in front. Anakin dived, timing his movement so that he was able to barely scoot underneath Hekula's Podracer and then rise up before the dip rose into a small hill.

He was in the lead. But Hekula had the next part of the course by now. He was most likely already planning his strategy for the next round of challenges. Anakin would have to rely on his instincts to keep him in the lead.

Behind him, Ody Mandrell couldn't make the sharp turn into the passage. Anakin heard the shriek of metal and the crash. Smoke rolled toward him and he pushed the engines as hard as he dared, trying to outrun the smoke before it blinded him.

Hekula was pulling slightly to the left. Anakin didn't know why but guessed he was preparing to pass him on the next segment . . . whatever it was. Just then the nav computer blinked, showing him the next part of the course. He just had time to register the details, but it was as though he had already seen the track.

He turned sharply on the first corner, then turned again to the left, then the right. Hekula kept up with his every move. Anakin could see his face when he glanced behind, could almost hear Hekula's cackling laugh.

Behind them, Elan and Aldar Beedo collided, after Elan made a move to cut off Aldar. The others had to scramble to avoid hitting them or the drivers, who had crawled from the wreckage to accuse each other. The sight was gone in a moment as Anakin whipped around another corner.

The controls shook in his hand at the constant turns. Hekula was gaining. He needed all his concentration for the next segment . . .

His comlink signaled.

Anakin considered not answering it, but he knew he must. It could be his Master.

He released the control for an instant and pressed

the activation key. He strained to hear his Master over the noise.

". . . nav computer . . . accident . . . prepare for . . ."

Anakin kept one hand on the controls and snatched the comlink. He held it tight against his ear. "Repeat!" he shouted into the comlink.

Now Obi-Wan's voice was clearer, but he still lost some words over the noise rebounding off the cave walls. "One of the Podracers is booby-trapped . . . nav computer will lead . . . Eusebus . . . the lead Podracer's steering mechanism will blow. It will be made to crash into a crowd . . . hear me, Anakin?"

"Copy that!" Anakin shouted. He threw the comlink back down.

The lapse in concentration had cost him. As his Podracer burst out of the maze, Hekula passed him on the inside and took the lead.

His nav computer flashed. The course now would wind through a series of turns, then open out into a large tunnel. Then the five remaining Podracers would burst out of the tunnel onto the city streets. So Obi-Wan's prediction was right.

Anakin quickly turned to the left before the cave wall curved. He was able to pass Hekula easily. Obviously, Hekula was not as adept a racer as his father. With advance knowledge of that turn, he should have hugged the wall to prevent Anakin's maneuver. Hekula tried to bump him from behind, but Anakin pulled ahead.

He raced through the tunnel, wondering what to do when he reached the city streets. If he slowed, the others would pass him, and there would be more danger to the pedestrians. The best he could do was stay ahead to lead the pack away from pedestrians and hope he could master the Podracer when its steering blew.

As Anakin zoomed onto the streets, he saw astonished faces and beings quickly running to get out of the way. He slowed slightly, but not enough to let Hekula pass him.

Suddenly Hekula pulled up next to him. He tried to use an old trick of his father's, flashing Anakin's engine with side vents so that he'd overheat. Anakin pulled ahead slightly to avoid the steam.

The next segment flashed onscreen. Down a boulevard, then up a steep hill and down the other side. The boulevard would then narrow into an alley, then open up once again.

The turn onto the boulevard would be tricky, a near-180-degree maneuver. Anakin eased to the right so he would be able to make the turn. Hekula kept going straight. When the turn appeared, Anakin took it easily, but Hekula had to struggle to keep his Podracer on course.

Engines screaming, they raced up the hill. Speeders accelerated to get out of their way, and pedestrians scattered. Anakin's hands began to shake, and he realized that his controls were vibrating. His warning light suddenly flashed red.

The steering mechanism was failing.

CHAPTER TWENTY

Obi-Wan had run off the edge of the platform and made a midair leap into the box of surprised VIP spectators. Then he dashed out into the stadium hall and was met by Siri.

"Not much excitement at the bowcaster skill event, so I thought I'd see how you were doing," she said. "I didn't realize you'd be competing."

Obi-Wan made the call to Anakin warning him about the steering mechanism. "We have to get down there."

"Where?" Siri pointed out. "We don't know where the Podracers will emerge from the caves. Nobody knows the track."

"Maxo Vista does."

They raced down to the exiting area, where Maxo Vista was hurrying off in disgrace. When he saw the

Jedi he tried to flee, but Siri took three strides forward and pinned him to a wall.

"Not so fast," she said. "We have some questions for you."

"I don't have anything to say." Maxo Vista's eyes burned with hatred for Obi-Wan.

Siri reached into Vista's tunic pocket. "We'll let your datapad do the talking."

She tossed the datapad to Obi-Wan and he quickly accessed Vista's files. Obi-Wan felt the urgency as he called up holofile after holofile, but his hands were steady and his eyes never stopped moving.

"Here," he said. "Here is the route. The steering mechanism will fail after the hill."

"Does it say which Podracer will be affected?" Siri asked.

"No." Even as he was speaking, he was contacting Anakin. "After the steep hill," he said quickly into his comlink, "the steering mech —"

"I know!" Anakin shouted. "It's mine! I can't —"

Anakin's words were drowned out by a loud crash and the comlink went dead.

Maxo Vista smiled. "It appears you were too late."

The crash occurred between Gargano and Zanales, who had been closely tailing Anakin and Hekula. Anakin did not look back to make sure that no one was hurt. He was too busy trying to bypass the steering mechanism. He guessed that it had been wired to blow through the nav computer.

He was controlling the Podracer through the engines now, just managing to keep it on course. Hekula had zoomed ahead.

A crowd of spectators stood on a corner ahead, right after a sharp curve. Anakin saw clearly that he could not control the Podracer on that turn. There was only one thing to do.

He shut off the nav computer to send the energy to the engines. He would have to rely on the Force.

Immediately the steering hummed with power again. He pushed the engines and in a burst of speed made the turn and cut Hekula off. He was in the lead again.

Slowing his speed just a fraction, he glanced in his rearview mirror. Hekula was going to attempt to pass him. Anakin would allow him to do so. He'd need to follow Hekula now. He had to let Hekula guide him to the finish line, then find a way to get ahead. His first objective was to protect the spectators, but Anakin had not forgotten for a moment that he meant to win.

Now he did not have to worry about injuring anyone. He had solved the problem of the steering. He just had to follow the course. His comlink activated again, but it was on the floor of the Podracer. He could not bend down to retrieve it. He would lose precious seconds. Now Anakin was focused on only one thing: the need to win.

"I'm sure he is all right, but you might as well go to the finish line," Siri said when Anakin didn't answer. "I'll stay with Vista."

"Bring him to the Ruling Power," Obi-Wan said. He knew Anakin was all right. He had to believe he would feel it if it weren't so. "I'll contact you after Anakin finishes the race."

Maxo Vista smirked as Siri led him away. "Good luck!" he called cheerily to Obi-Wan.

Obi-Wan hurried out of the stadium. He would have to get to the finish line on a swoop or speeder. It would be the fastest way to travel.

Astri was waiting outside, her eyes searching the crowd anxiously. She waved at Obi-Wan and pointed to a speeder by her side.

"Is everything all right? Is Maxo Vista involved?" she asked.

"I'm afraid so. Siri is taking him to the Ruling Power," Obi-Wan said.

Astri handed him a small viewscreen. Obi-Wan could

see the three Podracers roaring through the streets of Eusebus.

"They are selling these on the streets," she said. "Anakin seemed to have trouble, but he's in second place now."

Obi-Wan nodded, taking the viewscreen and jumping into the speeder.

She put her hand on the speeder for a moment. "Vista used Bog. Bog admired him."

Obi-Wan nodded. "Bog will be all right. He just needs to tell the truth."

Biting her lip, she nodded.

Obi-Wan took off. His comlink signaled, and he answered it.

"I have information for you on those Senators," Jocasta Nu said. "They aren't on a committee together. But they have all taken the same position on the same issue. The Commerce Guild is proposing legislation that would give them control of banking practices in the Core Worlds. It is an enormously profitable contract."

"Do the Senators oppose it?"

"Of course. It's a terrible idea to consolidate power that way," Jocastu Nu answered. "Rumor has it that many have been bribed to support it. The vote will be close. But the list of Senators you gave me have sworn to block it."

"Are the Ruling Power of Euceron involved?"

"No. But don't you want to know who is a member of the Commerce Guild?"

"Maxo Vista?"

"Indeed," Jocasta Nu said, sounding disappointed that Obi-Wan had guessed. "He was recently invited to join. Do you know who proposed his candidacy?"

"No, and I don't have time to guess —"

"Liviani Sarno."

Obi-Wan let out a breath. So his worst suspicions were true. The treachery had begun at the top. The Commerce Guild would do anything to ensure that the legislation would pass. As head of the Games Council, Liviani Sarno was in the perfect position to concoct a scheme to discredit the Senators who opposed it. Eager to join the Guild, no doubt Maxo Visto had agreed to take part.

No wonder Liviani Sarno had been so concerned about the theft of Bog's speeder. She knew the information on Bog's datapad could be traced back to her once the bats were discovered.

He ended the communication and concentrated on getting to the finish line as fast as he could. He would not feel easy until he saw Anakin cross the line, safe.

He contacted Siri. "Don't let Liviani Sarno interfere," he told her. "She may have been the one behind everything."

"I haven't seen her," Siri said. "But Vista seems pleased about something. That must be it. He must think Sarno will save him."

Obi-Wan returned to his piloting. He was almost at the caves now. It was strange how he had pulled a thread, and the plot had come undone. Didi's bet had led to a web of treachery. It never failed to surprise him, just a little, how far beings would go to advance their interests, how much they would risk for an easy gain. Together Liviani Sarno and Maxo Vista had wealth and prestige, yet it was not enough. And poor Aarno Dering, just a petty criminal with nothing to lose except his life. Obi-Wan thought back on his few possessions, his neat quarters. Dering was probably hoping to have enough credits to support himself for the rest of his life. No doubt he had taken pride in what he did. Obi-Wan thought back on the two chronos, set for morning. Dering must have been good at his job. He knew the importance of backup.

He knew the importance of backup.

Obi-Wan grabbed the screen and peered at it as he drove. Anakin was staying close to the rear of Hekula's Podracer. He tried to contact him on his comlink, but Anakin did not answer.

Answer it, Padawan. You know it is me.

Obi-Wan contacted Ry-Gaul. "Something else is going to happen to Anakin's Podracer," he said.

"The Force is still disturbed," Ry-Gaul agreed.

"Where are the most spectators?"

"At the finish line. I am there."

"That's where it will happen. I'll be there soon."

Obi-Wan pushed the engines to maximum. The boulevard ended and he zoomed along a dusty road, then over to the rolling hills. He remembered exactly where the cave entrance was and barely reduced speed as he crashed through the branches and slid into the tunnel.

He halted the speeder in the pit hangar. Groups of Pit Droids, mechanics, and members of the Podracing teams were crowded well clear of the finish line, view-screens in hand. He spotted Doby and Deland.

"He's still second," Doby fretted. "He's not going to win. And it looked like he almost crashed. I don't understand this!"

"All we can do is wait," Deland said, with a glance at his sister.

Sebulba had already called to Djulla to break out the food and drink for the celebration. He leaned over, watching his viewscreen avidly. "That's my boy!" he cackled. "Smash them all!"

Ry-Gaul, Tru, and Ferus approached Obi-Wan.

"We can do nothing now," Ry-Gaul said.

Obi-Wan scanned the crowd. Each being was staring

intently at a viewscreen. Some crowded around one small screen, others shared with one or two friends. He had to be right. There had to be someone who would activate the backup system by hand.

One being sat alone. A plain brown robe swept down to the floor. A hood hid a face bent intently over a viewscreen. Then a hand moved to reach inside the robe toward a pocket. A datapad appeared. In that brief movement Obi-Wan glimpsed a robe underneath the plain brown cloak. The color was brilliant scarlet and the thick veda cloth was embroidered with orange sept-silk thread.

Obi-Wan took off. He hurdled over some Pit Droids coiling a lubrication hose and avoided a disabled Pod-racer being wheeled into a transport. Startled gazes followed him as he rushed toward the seats.

The noise of the Podracers suddenly echoed through the caves. They were close. The spectators stood.

He knew, even as he ran, that he was too late. His throat constricted with pain.

Liviani Sarno touched the screen on her datapad, then slipped it back into a pocket. She quickly rose and jumped to the floor, hurrying away from the stands. She kept the viewscreen in front of her so she could keep her eye on the Podracers.

Obi-Wan took a quick look at his own viewscreen. They were close, racing now down a straightaway. There was one sharp turn right before the spectator stands, and then a short distance to the finish line.

He strode forward and put his hand on Sarno's arm. She looked up at him, surprised and, for a moment, frightened.

"I'll take that datapad," he said.

"What are you doing?" Liviani hissed. "I am here undercover. I am observing. Go away."

"What did you just do?"

"Nothing," she said, her eyes on the screen as the Podracers raced down the last straightaway. She struggled to get away. "Let me go!"

"If you did nothing, why are you so afraid?" Obi-Wan asked. The Podracers approached the last curve. He kept his hand on her wrist.

"Let me go!" Liviani screamed, her eyes wide with fear.

It is up to you now, Anakin. I failed to stop her. I cannot help you. There is only the Living Force.

Anakin was on a straightaway, but he knew his steering had failed completely as soon as it happened. He knew his braking system had shorted as well. The warning lights stayed green. No red lights flashed. The

Podracer did not wobble or shift. But the Force had gathered like a sudden storm cloud and filled his vision. He could see clearly and yet he knew the cloud was there.

This time the problem would not be easy to fix. It had not happened through the nav computer. He flipped switch after switch, but some kind of override had been programmed into his Podracer.

The turn was ahead. He was still hugging Hekula's tail. He had been preparing to make his move and pass him just before the turn. Now he knew he'd never make it. Instead, the Podracer would not turn. It would go out of control and crash into the stands.

He felt the Force around him and in him. In moments like this, Anakin felt capable of anything. The Force was like a gifted companion, a far-seeing guide, a power that gave his muscles strength and his mind and heart vision and will. He felt at the center of the moving Force. Ready.

There was only one thing to do, and he knew it. He saw the steps ahead that he needed to take. He saw the difficulties and the odds. He even saw the possibility of his own death. It did not matter.

He made his move. He slammed himself against the side of the Podracer and pushed the engine so that he maneuvered close to the left side of the tunnel wall.

Then he accelerated and came up neck and neck with Hekula on his right. Engines screaming, he was less than a centimeter from being smashed against the cave wall.

Hekula shot him an incredulous glance. It was as though Anakin was inside his mind. Hekula could take the opportunity to make one quick swipe, forcing him against the cave wall, and Anakin would be a fireball in seconds. But if Hekula did that, Neluenf, who was close behind them, would swing out to the right and no doubt win the race.

Revenge or victory? Anakin had bet on the answer.

Hekula did not turn his Podracer to sideswipe Anakin. Instead, he began the turn. Victory was too close for him to take the chance. Anakin's Podracer was so snug against Hekula's that it was forced to turn left as well. Sparks flew as his Podracer scraped along the wall.

The shell of the Podracer began to smoke. Anakin tasted smoke and fire in his mouth. He did not let up on his speed. If he did, he would be dead.

The spectators gasped as the two Podracers rounded the left curve, seemingly one connected beast. The flat straightaway was ahead, the finish line crowded with the Podracer teams and spectators who had risked the anger of Podracer security and jumped out of the stands.

And there was his Master, looking straight at him. The Podracer was barreling toward him at 600 kilometers an hour. And he had no brakes.

Anakin pushed the speed, passing Hekula. Then he cut the power and slammed all his weight to one side.

His Podracer began to spin. He crossed the finish line, spinning so wildly that neither Hekula or Neluenf could pass him.

The Podracer came to a slow stop. At first Anakin could not hear the cheers over the ringing in his ears.

He had won. And no one was dead.

Suddenly, he felt very tired. He saw the faces as a blur. Liviani Sarno, looking strangely pale. His Master, looking grave but relieved. And Sebulba, snarling at him, waving his arms and crying "Foul!"

Hot anger spilled through Anakin. He threw off his goggles and vaulted out of the Podracer.

"You!" he thundered at Hekula and Sebulba. "You're the cheats!"

Because of them, countless innocent beings might have been killed. Anakin had no doubt that Sebulba had been the one behind the sabotage of Deland's Podracer. They could not completely rely on getting the track information first. They had to destroy their closest rival. It was just like Sebulba to go that one, cruel step further.

The red mist he had come to recognize as rage filled his vision, driving out the memory of the clarity of the Force. He could see nothing but his rage against Sebulba, at anyone who would risk so many lives just to win.

"Slave boy! You have to cheat to win! There's no mother watching this time to disapprove!"

The taunting words filled his head and the red mist grew dense and hot.

He reached down for his lightsaber, but a strong hand closed over his.

"No, Padawan."

Obi-Wan's voice reached him as if from a long distance.

"He did it." Anakin struggled to keep the rage away. He pictured the red mist leaving him, floating over a distant hill. "He deserves to be punished."

"No." Obi-Wan's voice was stronger still. He drew Anakin away. "Listen to me, Padawan. Sebulba did not cheat. It was Doby and Deland."

Anakin blinked. He could not absorb the words. "It was . . ."

"They made a deal with Maxo Vista. They would have advance knowledge of the Podrace track. What they didn't know was that Vista was going to sabotage the Podracer. He wanted a fireball, a tremendous accident to occur."

"That means that . . . *I* was getting advance track information, not Hekula," Anakin said slowly. "It wasn't just the Force." That explained Hekula's sometimes puzzling failure to get ahead. He looked around. "Where are they?"

"They've disappeared with Djulla," Obi-Wan said. "I am sure they did it to save their sister. She has been freed, and they are gone. They most likely hid a transport nearby."

Sebulba was still watching him. Hekula sat slumped in his Podracer, too stunned to emerge. "You'll pay for this, slave boy!" Sebulba snarled.

Anakin took a step toward him but again his Master stopped him.

"He is my enemy," Anakin said.

"You are a Jedi," Obi-Wan told him. His voice was low and pitched only for Anakin. "You are a Jedi," he repeated.

The mist in Anakin's head cleared. He took a breath and looked around. Ferus Olin was watching him, as he always was, his dark eyes gleaming with secret knowledge, as if he had glimpsed the red mist that was Anakin's rage. Tru nodded at him, his expression showing only loyalty and affection. Ry-Gaul appeared to be guarding Liviani Sarno.

Nothing was as he thought it would be. He felt his legs trembling. He had almost lost control in front of his fellow Padawans and two Jedi Masters. He had come so close.

Obi-Wan's voice was gentle. "Come, Padawan. There is a mission to complete."

CHAPTER TWENTY-ONE

The hearing was presided over by Ruler Three, Ruler Six, and Ruler Seven. The entire Games Council was allowed to attend.

Obi-Wan was not allowed to hear the testimony before his. It was how hearings were conducted on Euceron. He watched Maxo Vista emerge, then Liviani Sarno, then Bog. At last he was called.

Obi-Wan laid out the details of what he had discovered. He accused Liviani Sarno and Maxo Vista of conspiring to disgrace the Senators in order for the Commerce Guild to pass legislation that would earn them fortunes beyond measure. He accused Maxo Vista specifically of the murder of Aarno Dering.

"Have you evidence of this?" Ruler Three asked.

"The files on Liviani Sarno's and Maxo Vista's datapads were timed to erase themselves," Obi-Wan admitted. "And no one saw Maxo Vista run away from Dering but me."

"Did you see his face?"

"No," Obi-Wan said. "He wore a concealing helmet. Yet I knew it was him."

"So we have only your word that the hero of Euceron and the illustrious head of the Games are guilty," Ruler Three said.

"My word is all you need," Obi-Wan answered.

"Perhaps on Coruscant," Ruler Three said coolly. "But not on Euceron. You claim that the Podracer was programmed to crash into a crowd. But it did not crash."

"Only thanks to the skill of my Padawan."

"You claim Aarno Dering fixed three events, yet Aarno Dering is dead. Maxo Vista and Liviani Sarno have denied all charges. The Games Council has backed them up."

"Didi Oddo can confirm the events were fixed —"

"He has left the planet."

That was not a surprise. "Bog Divinian saw the files on Vista's datapad," Obi-Wan said.

"He has denied seeing them," Ruler Seven said.

Obi-Wan remembered Bog's sad notes on how to succeed. NEVER CONTRADICT A SUPERIOR!! FOLLOW THE POWER!!

He had been foolish to imagine that Bog would not give in to pressure from Maxo and Liviani.

He gazed at the faces of the Council. None of them met his eyes. No one wanted the scandal to see the light. Not the Ruling Power, not the Games Council. And no doubt Bog Divinian had just ensured that he would be elected Senator on his homeworld. The Commerce Guild would see to that.

This is what the galaxy is becoming, Obi-Wan thought with a sudden, sharp sadness. *Those with power hide the truth, and the weak go along in hopes they will become the strong.*

"I can see there is no more I can do here," Obi-Wan said. He strode off the platform and left the room.

Anakin was waiting. When he told him what had occurred, his Padawan was furious. "How can they do this? Maxo Vista and Liviani Sarno are guilty! And they are going to walk free! This is an injustice!" Anakin's words echoed off the hard plastoid walls of the Grand Court.

"It is a hard thing to see happen," Obi-Wan agreed. "But sometimes even when the mission is successful, justice is not done. It happens. At least the Commerce Guild did not get what they wanted. No spectators were killed and their legislation may be defeated by those they wished to disgrace."

"And Aarno Dering? Maxo Vista will get away with murder!"

"That is the hardest of all," Obi-Wan said.

They walked down the hall toward the exit. As they pushed through the heavy metal doors, they saw Astri waiting, leaning against the rail. She came toward them slowly.

"I am sorry, Obi-Wan," Astri said. "I offered to testify, but I didn't see the datapad myself, so the Ruling Power would not allow me. It was my word against Bog's. Didi wanted to help, but Bog said he would press charges for the theft of the speeder. So Didi thought it best to leave the planet. You know he has no moral courage." Astri shook her head. "I seem to have married a similar man. Bog isn't bad. He was pressured by Liviani and he worships Maxo Vista. He swears to me that when he becomes Senator he will do good."

Obi-Wan nodded sadly. "I'm sure he believes that, Astri. But he is already in debt before he starts. He has done a favor for the Commerce Guild, but he has lied in a hearing. So they have something on him. That will corrupt him."

"I am frightened for my future," Astri said, her dark eyes bleak. "But I have no choice but to go on."

Obi-Wan touched her cheek. "Your loyalty is what drives you, Astri. I would not like to see you lose that."

"So we are still friends?"

"We will always be friends."

Astri nodded and slowly walked down the steps. Soon she was lost in the swirl of the crowd. Obi-Wan felt a sudden pang. Would he ever see her again?

"Nothing has turned out as I thought," Anakin said. "I was here to work on my Jedi lesson of connection to the Living Force. If that is true, I've failed. I judged everyone wrong. I did not see that Doby and Deland were using me. I trusted my instincts, and they betrayed me."

"Do not judge yourself so harshly, Padawan," Obi-Wan said. "Your mistake was one of the heart. You allowed your emotion to cloud your instincts. You allowed what your heart *wanted* to be true to make it true. Connections to other beings, good and bad, must be pure and free of one's own desires. You *wanted* Sebulba to be the culprit, so you made him one."

"I thought my connection to the Living Force was clear, and it's not at all," Anakin said moodily. "I have such a long way to go."

"If it makes you feel better, I made the same mistake with Maxo Vista," Obi-Wan said. "Jedi lessons are learned by Masters as well as Padawans."

"Wisdom comes with time and missions," Anakin said, repeating Obi-Wan's own words.

Obi-Wan smiled gently. "And mistakes," he said.